D1559708

SHERLOCK HOLMES AND THE ALICE IN WONDERLAND MURDERS

Center Point
Large Print

Also by Barry Day and available from
Center Point Large Print:

*Sherlock Holmes and the
Shakespeare Globe Murders*

SHERLOCK HOLMES
AND THE
ALICE IN WONDERLAND
MURDERS

BARRY DAY

CENTER POINT LARGE PRINT
THORNDIKE, MAINE

The text of this Large Print edition is unabridged.
In other aspects, this book may vary
from the original edition.
Printed in the United States of America
on permanent paper.
Set in 16-point Times New Roman type.

ISBN: 978-1-68324-403-5

Library of Congress Cataloging-in-Publication Data

Names: Day, Barry, author.
Title: Sherlock Holmes and the Alice in Wonderland murders / Barry
Day.
Description: Center Point Large Print edition. | Thorndike, Maine :
Center Point Large Print, 2017.
Identifiers: LCCN 2017008786 | ISBN 9781683244035
   (hardcover : alk. paper)
Subjects: LCSH: Holmes, Sherlock—Fiction. | Watson, John H.
(Fictitious character)—Fiction. | Private investigators—England—
Fiction. | Murder—Investigation—Fiction. | Large type books. | GSAFD:
Mystery fiction.
Classification: LCC PR6054.A928 S54 2017 | DDC 823/.914—dc23
LC record available at https://lccn.loc.gov/2017008786

This one is for Elinor . . .

CHAPTER ONE

I can't honestly say I've ever thought of myself as much of a fisherman. In fact, put me behind a rod and line and I find I'm closer to Isaac Newton contemplating the universe than Isaak Walton trying to outwit some benighted bass or sturgeon or whatever. Which is why I confess myself surprised to receive Holmes's telegram.

> "MY DEAR FELLOW STOP NEED YOU
> ON SCOTTISH FISHING EXPEDITION
> STOP COME IF CONVENIENT IF NOT
> COME ANYWAY STOP SH."

I must admit the prospect of sitting on some yon bonnie bank with the Scots mist finding the chinks in my ulster didn't precisely fire my imagination but the prospect of seeing my old friend more than compensated for that. I had long nourished a shrewd suspicion that he regarded me as just as much of a fixture in his life as his pipe, his violin, his cuttings books—even his smelly old chemical apparatus. Equally, I knew that he wouldn't willingly give up one of them, if he had the choice.

In any case, I was content to be a part of the furniture that occasionally came to life for him.

My practice—if one could call it that—had not really received my full attention for some time. If the truth be told, I found it rather dull after some of the more bizarre little episodes Holmes and I had been through together since his return from what he ironically referred to as the Great Moriarty Hiatus a couple of years earlier.

I had another reason for welcoming his invitation, characteristically unvarnished though it might be. But then, I had long since given up expecting the irrelevant trappings society commonly expected. In the time since his "renaissance" he had thrown himself into his work with feverish energy. It was almost as though he felt he had to run twice as fast to catch up the time he had lost and, indeed, the criminal population of the metropolis were already counting the cost. In the spring of the previous year—summoning up as much gravitas as I felt he would accept—I advised him as his medical man, as well as his friend, that he must take a break or risk a complete breakdown. I could see that my professional opinion left him unmoved but my final argument was what clinched matters.

"Wouldn't it be ironic," I mused aloud, "if you were to put *yourself* out of action when the good Professor so singularly failed?"

A week later we were ensconced in Poldhu Bay, a small village on the Cornish coast, where I did my best to keep the world at bay. There was, it must be admitted, one brief interruption, when Holmes was called upon to solve a rather irritating case of multiple murder by exotic poison—which I intend to write up one of these days under the working title of *The Adventure of the Devil's Foot.* Even now I can hear him muttering about another of my "lurid tales"—but so be it! I have heard him refer to the affair as the "Cornish Horror" from his own lips.

"The strangest case I have ever handled, Watson."

That aside—and perhaps because of it—for a brief while I was able to get him to relax as much as someone of his hyperactive nature is capable of doing. But now, a short year later, I could see the signs recurring. The tension in the muscles of that angular jaw, the constant tapping of those steepled fingers in front of his face as he sat before the empty summer fireplace in Baker Street, his head wreathed in the smoke generated by the noxious shag he insisted on smoking—all these signs betokened a man with his mainspring too tightly coiled.

I had been wracking my brains to come up with another ruse to distract him when Holmes solved the problem for me with his telegram. He had disappeared in his typically mysterious fashion a few days earlier and I knew enough by now not to worry and to wait his pleasure. I had always found plenty to occupy my time in our great city. In fact, so busy was I with one thing and another that it was a trifle inconvenient to leave London at such short notice. But since it was so clearly a question of *carpe diem*, I did precisely that. Fortunately, my military experience had at least made enforced travelling second nature and my needs are few. Which is why I then found myself that mid-October afternoon in 1898, my worst fears justified, sitting on a large damp rock on the shore of an apparently endless Scottish loch. If the water harboured fish, it was certainly hoarding them with true Scots parsimony and my principal activity these past several hours had been an unsuccessful attempt to hold my rod steady and keep my pipe dry at the same time. To add injury to insult the damp was causing the old war wound from that infernal Jezail bullet to play up.

The loch itself was shrouded with mist, as it had been for each of the three days we had been there. It was one of those mists that part and meet like theatre curtains opening and closing, giving tantalising glimpses of the far shore and distorting sounds. Someone of a poetical nature would no doubt wax lyrical about its dreamlike, ethereal quality but for me the persistent drizzle was all too real.

Holmes had long since given up the pleasures of rod and line and taken himself off along the shore line. This, I might add, surprised me less than the fact that we were there in the first place.

Over the years I had heard him frequently express the view that neither the country nor the sea presented the slightest attraction to him, yet here we were, up to our ears in both! In fact, as the days had gone by, I had received the clear impression that fishing was strictly secondary on whatever agenda he had devised for himself. As long as he was away from Baker Street and the endless round of trivial pursuits—what he once referred to dismissively as "recovering lead pencils and giving advice to young ladies from boarding schools"—I was not about to complain. Or, at least, not about that.

At that moment the subject of my reverie materialised. Wearing the long travelling cloak and the close-fitting cloth cap that was his invariable attire when out of town, he was an impressively spectral sight as he parted the curtain of mist and appeared at my side. It was on the tip of my tongue to enquire whether he had enjoyed his solitary perambulation when something about his expression, now that I could see it, made me hold my peace. That all-too-familiar concentration in his gaze told me he had reached some point of decision. Before I could question him, a sharp tug on my line almost took the rod out of my hand.

"Good heavens, Holmes," I cried, "I do believe . . ."

And then, to my amazement, that infuriating

man snatched it from my hand and cast it on the ground.

"No time for that, Watson," I heard him say, as he took me by the elbow and propelled me through the mist towards the track that had brought us there from the nearby inn where we were staying. "We have other fish to fry." And as the mist once more enshrouded us, I heard a peal of ghostly laughter.

A few minutes later bowling along in the trap we had hired for our stay he had the grace to come as near to an apology as I was likely to receive.

"I'm afraid I've been a little preoccupied these last few days, old fellow," he said. And then, patting me briefly on my affronted arm—"Don't worry. Tonight I shall stand you the freshest trout and the coldest Chablis mine host can provide. Perhaps even a few oysters. There is, you will no doubt have observed, an 'R' in the month. And by the by, the fishing in the river that runs by the inn is in every way superior to the overgrown pond that was occupying your afternoon's efforts."

Before I could point out that the "pond" had been at his insistence, he went on: "And as for the rod . . . top of the line at the Army & Navy Stores what—five? six?—years ago . . . briefly lent to an old army friend . . . left handed . . . a former gunner, unless I miss my mark, now somewhat arthritic in the forefinger . . . don't worry about that. I'll have the boy from the inn go straight back and retrieve it. The fish, too, if he's lucky."

He took his eye off the track to give me a sidelong glance knowing full well he had me hooked as tightly as I'd had that fish, which would grow in size with every retelling. On this occasion I felt I had indulged him enough for one afternoon, so after a pause he continued— "Not being one of nature's predators but an amateur in the true sense of the word, when you bought a rod, you would naturally buy the best and since the Army & Navy draws you like a homing pigeon . . . You are right-handed yet the wear on the—what do you call it?—the handle clearly indicates a left-handed person. And then the wear marks are uneven, indicating the user was not exerting the usual pressure on the finger most of us rely on . . ."

At that point I capitulated, as he knew I would.

"Yes, yes, elementary, my dear Holmes," I said, imitating his distinctive voice as best I could, "but how did you know about old Tug being in the Engineers . . . ?"

"A man may rise to the highest rank, Watson, but he will never entirely rid his nostrils of the smell of cordite nor his fingers from ingrained gunpowder. But enough of my parlour tricks. Watson, I confess I have been less than candid with you. The purpose of our little trip was not fishing . . ."

"That," I said with as much irony as I could muster, "I had deduced for myself."

"No," Holmes continued, as though I had not spoken, "there is a party I am anxious to attend."

"A party?" Anyone less social than my old friend would be hard to imagine.

"You've dragged me to this godforsaken spot for a *party?*"

Before I could vent my frustrations any further, something about his expression caught my eye. His face was turned in profile to me and instinctively I recalled how in times of crisis he would never make eye contact with me. It was as though to do so would break his concentration.

An anaemic sun was trying to break through the mist and it illuminated that distinctive aquiline profile that could so easily have adorned a Roman coin. The gaze was focused somewhere just beyond the apparent horizon. I prepared to listen to what he had to say, for I knew it was not idle chatter.

"You and I are about to be uninvited guests at what I believe is called a Press Party. Our host will be one John Moxton . . ."

"That newspaper chap who's causing all the fuss?"

"The very same, Watson. Since he arrived from America just over two years ago with apparently unlimited resources, Mr. Moxton has—according to his admittedly jealous rivals in Fleet Street—

undermined the very foundations of serious journalism as we know it."

"Foundations built on sand, if I'm any judge," I interrupted. "Why some of the things I've read in the popular press lately would shock my maiden aunt . . ."

"If you *had* a maiden aunt—which to the best of my knowledge you do not. Nonetheless, your sentiments are shared by many, old fellow. Not that I can claim to be anything of an expert in matters journalistic. As you well know, I read nothing but the police reports and the agony columns. As far as human aspiration and misery are concerned, they more than suffice. However, supposing Fleet Street is in need of a shake up, then this man is in the process of administering it."

A recollection came to me. "Didn't his paper—what's it called? The *Clarion*? run those articles on parliamentary indiscretions over the ages?"

"*Commons Ladies*—a series of interviews with women who claimed to have had liaisons with Members of Parliament? Quite right, Watson. Not that you actually *read* them, of course. But the clever thing was that Moxton's justification for the piece lay in the fact of aristocratic indiscretion as a British tradition going back to King Charles and Nell Gwynne and even further. And he does the same thing with all of his *exposés*, as he calls them. The public's right to know. In one of them he even quotes the American Constitution and freedom of speech . . . In another he argues that comparable Presidential dalliances are rendered impossible because of the puritanical influence of the Founding Fathers. I wonder . . ."

"Then why doesn't the fellow go back to America or wherever he came from?" I demanded. "I'm afraid I don't have too much patience with people who come over trying to change things that have worked perfectly well for longer than some of these countries have *been* countries."

Holmes, however, was not to be distracted from his theme: "What friend Moxton seems to have hit on is the fact that there is a new and reasonably literate middle class emerging who want to be talked to in their own idiom and not talked down to. When Moxton talks about the 'popular press' from one of his soap boxes—and you'll notice the man is quoted constantly in his own paper, as if he were some kind of messiah—he strikes an emotional chord with a lot of people. I believe such men can be forces for good or ill but, being a pessimist by nature—as you know better than anyone, Watson—I suspect their motives. So much power can so easily corrupt those it touches. I am anxious to study the first of the species to emerge on our shores. I very much doubt that he will be the last. Ah, here we are . . ."

CHAPTER TWO

The trap turned into what must originally have been a large meadow that led down to the shores of the loch. On a day in high summer I imagine it must have been pleasant for the locals to picnic here but the sight that met our eyes was very different.

A large marquee had been erected, open to the water and a temporary flooring of planks had been laid, largely covered with what seemed to my untutored eye some rather valuable carpets. I spotted at least a couple of designs that seemed vaguely familiar from my days in the Raj. Clearly, no expense had been spared for this occasion— whatever it happened to be.

Circulating around this elegantly improvised drawing room were some hundred or so equally elegant people, while moving unobtrusively among them were almost as many flunkeys in formal uniform dispensing flutes of champagne and canapés. It was, to say the least, not a sight one would have expected to see in this remote spot.

Holmes resolved at least one of the questions going through my mind when he murmured: "Our friend Moxton hired a special train, I believe, to transport his guests here for the occasion."

"Yes, Holmes," I murmured in reply, "but what is the occasion, pray?"

Before my friend could answer, there was a sharp tinkling sound of a spoon or fork tapping the side of a glass, which quickly silenced the chatter of conversation. All eyes turned to the edge of the room nearest the water, where a tall grey haired man had moved into a space where he could command his audience. Instinctively, those nearest drew back to give him room and, indeed, there was something about his presence which seemed to demand deference.

He may have been an inch or so over six feet but his general bearing and the immaculate cut of what was obviously an expensive suit—tailored, I observed, thanks to Holmes's persistent training in the rather more relaxed style of our North American cousins—gave the impression of a much bigger man.

Come to think of it, though, it was less his build than his eyes that dominated that assembly. Piercing and almost coal black, they shone forth from bushy white brows, leaving everyone in the room, I felt sure, with the same impression they created on me, that he had sought them out for his undivided attention. I suddenly realised that I had only seen one other pair of eyes remotely like them in my life—and they belonged to the man standing next to me.

"Good afternoon, ladies and gentlemen," he was

18

saying as two flunkeys placed a small podium in front of him, so that he could lean at his ease while addressing his guests. "My name is John Moxton and for my sins I run this little news sheet some of you may be familiar with."

Here he held up a newspaper that had been lying on the podium. There was a ripple of polite laughter from his guests. I had seen his "little news sheet" before, of course, on the vendors' stands as I went about my business but it had never crossed my mind to purchase it. My *Daily Chronicle* kept me abreast of the world's woes and, if I needed further bad news, the *Evening Standard* would inform me of the further damage our four legged friends were inflicting on my Army pension. This was the first occasion I had had to actually study it and I have to say, my instinctive fears were justified.

It didn't even look like a real newspaper. The thing was almost square and the banner *The Clarion* was certainly aptly named for, together with its symbol of a hand raised to an open mouth, it seemed to take up an inordinate amount of the front page. Below it was an even larger headline—CAN BRITANNIA RULE?—and a rather unflattering portrait of Her Majesty. The whole thing, to my mind, was in distinctly questionable taste and I was about to say so to Holmes when Moxton continued . . .

"In the two short years of our existence I think

I can say we have made ourselves noticed . . ."

He smiled to show that he meant the remark humorously and there was another ripple of laughter around the tent.

"You'll notice I didn't say liked?" A louder ripple.

"Our clarion call—or should I say, our *Clarion* call is—'Let Truth Be Heard!' And Truth, I'm afraid, is not always either pretty or popular. Either way, the people have the right to know it. But don't let me get carried away on my favourite topic on such a festive occasion . . ."

As he smiled again, you could feel his audience responding to him and I was reminded of a favourite preacher with his congregation. This man had the makings of a demagogue.

"Today we are here—and thank you to all of you for taking the time out of your busy lives. I think I even see the faces of some of our friendly Fleet Street competitors, do I not? As I say, today we are here to try and tease one of her secrets out of Mother Nature."

Here he indicated with a sweep of his arm the expanse of water behind him. As if on cue the mist had started to lift and now we could see that the loch seemed to stretch to infinity. The late afternoon light played tricks with perspective and the ripples on the surface were hypnotic if you looked at them long enough. It was only then that the truth struck me.

"Of course!" I muttered before Holmes nudged me into silence. Now I knew where we were. In my haste to get here I had taken the train to Inverness and then the pony and trap to the inn Holmes had specified, all without studying the map. The loch I had been fishing in to so little effect these last few days was . . .

"Loch Ness," Moxton continued "has been the stuff of legend since the fifteenth century. The locals swear by The Great Beastie, the rest of the world has always been in more than two minds. Is it a legend of the Scots—or has it more to do with the Scotch?" Here he waited for and received the laughter he anticipated.

"Today the *Clarion* says 'Let Truth Be Heard'— and I've invited you all here to hear and see that truth, if truth it be. Is there indeed a Loch Ness Monster?"

He paused to let the murmur of speculation echo around the room, rather like the small waves from the loch on the nearby shore. I whispered to Holmes—"Surely the fellow hasn't brought all these people up here on an off chance? After all, there have only been a handful of so-called sightings in donkey's years . . ."

"This fellow, as you call him, does nothing by chance, old fellow. Be patient."

Having given his audience long enough to absorb his announcement, Moxton consulted a large gold fob watch.

"Five o'clock, as near as makes no difference, and my local friends tell me that this is Nessie's feeding time and that this particular spot in the loch is where most of the sightings have taken place in recent years. Now, some of you are probably saying to yourselves—'What makes this American madman think that the Beast—should there be a beast—will conveniently appear to suit our convenience?' A good question—to which I believe we have a good answer."

He indicated a dark complexioned middle-aged man at the front of the crowd, who looked as though he might have been more at home in the boxing ring. "Professor James here hails from the Oceanographic Institute in Boston, where they have been conducting some mighty interesting experiments with the use of sonar equipment in the tracking of shoals of fish. With the *Clarion*'s help"—and here he made the universal sign for money with the thumb and forefinger, which drew the expected laughter—"he has adapted that equipment in a way that we hope will engage the attention of our legendary friend."

By now the tension in the room was palpable. Even the other journalists Moxton had pointed out had dropped their pretence of being blasé. The man had all of us eating out of his hand. All of us, I should say, except one. As I turned to address my friend, I saw an expression on his face such as I have rarely observed. His eyes were blazing and the object of his gaze—John Moxton— seemed to pick up some sort of vibration, for he appeared momentarily uncomfortable and, I could almost swear, restrained himself from returning Holmes's stare. Instead, he turned to Professor James.

"Are you ready, Professor? Shall we . . . ?"

By now two of James's white-coated assistants had carried out a large metal box and set it up on a table where we could all see it. It had a variety of knobs and dials and several lengths of metal cable leading down into the water. James made a series of adjustments and then turned to nod to Moxton.

"Very well, then, ladies and gentlemen—supper time!"

On cue James threw a red switch and all eyes turned to the loch. You could hear the silence from the indrawn breath. And then—nothing. Moxton, it must be confessed, seemed to thrive on the heightened tension.

"Increase the voltage," he ordered and then, turning back to as rapt an audience as I have seen outside a theatre—"I should explain the principle of our little experiment The professor's machine is linked to a series of cells submerged in the loch at various depths and distances. The electric current sets off underwater vibrations inaudible to human ears but which we believe will be—shall we say—disconcerting to any aquatic species such as our friend, Nessie. By way of relief it is conjectured that the 'monster' will seek the surface, however briefly. Professor, if we may . . ."

This time James threw two switches, the red one and a green one. There was a silence in which the proverbial pin would have sounded like an avalanche and then . . .

"There! What's that?" There was the high-pitched squeal from an elderly lady to my left who looked as though she had never raised her voice higher than to ask for a second cup of tea. And then I swear the hair on the back of my neck rose, as I heard a sound more frightening than any that had reached my ears since that damned Dartmoor hound. It was low and reverberating and seemed to contain within it the pain of the world.

I could feel my own emotions echo around the makeshift room. And then out of the loch—perhaps two hundred yards away in the fading light—something rose from the water and was gone again.

Holmes is fond of telling me that I see but I do not observe but that image was burned into my brain right enough. It was dark, a sort of greyish black, and appeared scaly and shiny with the water running off it. Before I had time to do more than grip my friend by the arm, it appeared again a few yards further away. Or was that a second hump? The whole episode was over so quickly it was impossible to tell.

The room was in a state of pandemonium. It was like being in a human aviary. Finally Moxton stepped forward and raised both hands for silence.

"Ladies and gentlemen," he repeated until the hubbub had somewhat died down. "I hardly think we can expect our aquatic friend to entertain us further this evening, so I propose we leave him—or indeed her . . ." and he bowed courteously in the direction of the lady who had cried out first, earning a nervous laugh from his other guests. "I propose we leave—whatever—to enjoy its dinner without further interruption.

"Thank you for sharing this historic moment when a centuries old legend became fact. Tomorrow the *Clarion* will tell the world the truth about the Loch Ness Monster. And, as we newspaper folk like to say—you heard it here first! Now, ladies and gentlemen, please continue to enjoy yourselves and join me in a toast . . ."

As he spoke the servants were circulating with trays of filled champagne glasses. "To Nessie!"

"To Nessie!" the cry went up and then the decibel level rose again as the guests broke up into groups talking excitedly among themselves.

"Good heavens, Holmes," I said turning to my friend and taking a good gulp of Moxton's excellent champagne, "did you ever see anything like it?"

"No, old fellow," said Holmes, looking strangely sombre, "I don't believe I ever did."

"You mean one legend has managed to surprise another?"

The voice came from behind us and suddenly a heavy hand was briefly rested on both our shoulders. I sensed rather than saw my friend recoil involuntarily from unwelcome physical contact, then the hands were removed. We turned and found ourselves facing a small group with Moxton at the front of it.

"Forgive me, Mr. Holmes, I should have remembered to keep my cultural distance. You British require your personal space. It's something we New World *arrivistes* have still to learn."

"And I'm sure you will absorb it with the same impressive speed that characterises your entire enterprise," Holmes replied smoothly, offering his hand to the magnate, who hesitated for a moment, before shaking it warmly, using the American habit of covering their linked hands with his free one.

"Coming from you, sir, I choose to take that as a compliment, although I sense there may be a touch of that good old British irony lurking in there somewhere. And this, I have no doubt, is your good friend and associate, Dr. Watson . . . ?"

I was treated to the same handshaking routine. Now why, I wondered, was I left with the feeling that I was watching a carefully-orchestrated performance? Even the handshake seemed calculated in the degree of firmness one might

26

expect from an extrovert virile man. Then my social sense overcame my instinct and I let the thought drift away.

Moxton was now introducing the rest of his group. At his shoulder, like the lead dog in a pack, was a tall, slender man with a small moustache clipped short and glossy black hair slicked back and worn rather longer than the current fashion. Sleek was the only way to describe him, as if he had so designed himself that nothing should impede his forward progress. Even his features seemed to be questing and his eyes, I observed, were never still. Right now Holmes was the focus of his attention and it was as though he were devouring the man.

"Mr. Holmes—Dr. Watson—may I present my good friend and—if he doesn't mind my saying so—the *Clarion*'s new protégé, Mr. Royston Steel?"

When Moxton mentioned the name, the pieces suddenly fell into place and I knew where I had seen that face before. In the last few months that slightly reptilian stare—I could sense I wasn't going to warm to the fellow—had challenged the country from newspaper pages and poster hoardings alike, most particularly from the pages of the *Clarion*. I even remembered the slogan that accompanied it . . .

"THIS COUNTRY NEEDS A TOUCH OF STEEL!"

The first time I'd spotted it in my *Chronicle*, I'd complained to Holmes about the way these newspaper chappies were vulgarising our perfectly good language but he'd been too immersed in his favourite Agony Column to do more than mutter something about it being a living language or something such. Anyway, here was the man Britain apparently needed as large as life and for my money—as my old nanny used to say—twice as ugly.

I returned from my reverie to find Holmes and Steel exchanging what passed for pleasantries but I noticed Holmes distinctly did not offer his hand this time. Nor did Steel seem to expect it. My friend's personal space remained inviolate—until into it stepped one of the most beautiful women I had ever seen. It has always amused Holmes to tease me that "the fair sex is your department, Watson." I should never have made the mistake of boasting to him on one over-excited occasion that my experience of women extended over many nations and three separate continents. However, I suppose I have had my moments. Certainly, I have always been far from immune to a pretty face or a delicately turned ankle. But this young lady was what I believe might be called a *nonpareil*.

The face was a perfect oval but her beauty was not of that empty passive kind that only exists to be admired by others. Those eyes could sparkle and that mouth had humour etched into its corners. Her dark hair was loosely swept up now and held in place with an antique silver comb but, left to its own devices, would have cascaded down her back. I put her somewhere in her mid-twenties and was just wondering how Burne-Jones or Millais might have done justice to her on canvas, when I felt a tug on my sleeve.

"Have you forgotten your manners, Watson?" It was Holmes and I could see that he was smiling faintly for the first time since the encounter began.

"Mr. Moxton was just introducing us to his ward, Miss Alicia Creighton . . ."

Slightly flustered, I turned to take the small hand that was offered in my direction. For the briefest of moments her eyes met mine. They were a fine blue-grey but, instead of indulging myself in further admiration—as I fully expected—I experienced a shock of reality. This lady was deeply unhappy. It was something to do with the tiny gap between the look and the accompanying smile and then the sensation was gone. If I thought I was the only one to notice it, it soon became clear that Moxton at least was sensitive to the atmosphere, for he rapidly filled the conversational gap.

"Yes, Alicia is my sister's only child and when her folks unfortunately—well, we don't want to dwell on that, do we? Well, naturally, I took her under my wing . . ."

Was it my imagination or did the image cause Miss Creighton to shudder slightly? Moxton continued: "Not that we know each other all that well yet. Alicia's only been home from her travels for a few weeks but I think she's arrived in time for a little excitement. A lot is happening in this country, don't you agree, Mr. Holmes? As we say where I come from—'You ain't seen nuthin' yet'. And that's the truth . . ."

"Indeed, one sincerely hopes it will be the truth we shall see and hear, Mr. Moxton," Holmes replied. "But then, people have such different definitions of the word, don't you find?"

"'What is truth?' said Jesting Pilate . . ." Moxton declaimed the line like an actor in a voice loud enough to cause several other nearby guests to turn in our direction.

"'. . . and would not stay for an answer' was, I seem to recall, the end of Bacon's quotation," Holmes replied.

"A literary man, to add to your other accomplishments, I see, Mr. Holmes? This is too intriguing. May I test you with one more? 'When *I* use a word . . . it means just what I choose it to mean—neither more or less.'"

"Humpty Dumpty . . . 'The question is,' said Alice, 'whether you *can* make words mean so many different things.'"

"'"The question is," said Humpty Dumpty . . .'" And now Moxton looked positively triumphant—"'which is to be master—that's all.'"

Then, almost as if he felt he had given too much away, he added in a lower tone—"I see you are a fellow *aficionado* of the great—and recently late—Dodgson?"

"Dodgson?" I interrupted. "Who's Dodgson? I could have sworn that came from that fellow—what's his name?"

"Carroll, old fellow," Holmes came to my rescue. "Lewis Carroll, the *nom de plume* of the late—and, as Mr. Moxton rightly says, great—writer, Charles Lutwidge Dodgson, author of *Alice in Wonderland* and its sequel, *Alice Through the Looking Glass . . .*"

"I've often wondered why he chose that particular name. Perhaps you can enlighten me?"

This from Steel. "Elementary. Dodgson simply translated his first two names into Latin—'Carolus Lodovicus' and then anglicized them into 'Lewis Carroll'. He literally invented himself—a practice in which he was not the first nor, I suspect, will he be the last."

"Children's books, aren't they?" I was determined to retrieve a little lost ground with Miss Creighton watching.

"Ostensibly written for children, Watson, but in the eyes of many incidental works of somewhat surrealistic philosophy, indicating—among other things—that few things are what they seem."

"Well put, Mr. Holmes," Moxton added and seemed about to take the point further, when Steel—clearly not used to being silent when two or more were gathered together—interrupted . . .

"So, tell us, Mr. Holmes—what do you think of today's 'scoop'?"

Moxton, who had looked momentarily irritated at being cut off in full flow, now looked at Holmes with even greater intensity.

"Yes, Mr. Holmes, were you persuaded by the evidence of your own eyes? Or will you wait until tomorrow's headlines tell the world?"

Holmes paused for a moment to consider his reply. Then, looking Moxton squarely in the eye: "Watson will tell you that it has long been one of my maxims that the Press is a most valuable institution—if you only know how to use it. Having now met you, Mr. Moxton, I am left in no doubt that you of all people know precisely how to use it . . . Now, if you'll excuse us—Miss Creighton, Mr. Steel—until our paths cross again. Dr. Watson and I have a train to catch . . . Thank you for a most revealing afternoon. Goodbye, Mr. Moxton . . ."

"Oh, John, please, Mr. Holmes."

"You wouldn't prefer—James?"

I sensed a distinct frisson as Moxton paused a moment. "Aren't they one and the same thing? Goodbye, Mr. Holmes. I look forward to renewing our new acquaintance in the great metropolis."

• • •

A few minutes later we were in our trap—which seemed to me to be suspiciously ready for us— and leaving the marquee behind us, glowing now with candlelight in the gathering dusk.

"What's all this about a train, Holmes?"

"Oh, don't worry, Watson, your supper is safe enough. It was time to make a strategic withdrawal. Besides, there's something I want to show you before the light goes entirely."

"I should think I've seen quite enough for on day," I replied somewhat huffily.

Even after all these years it disconcerts me have my routine disturbed quite so forcibly. If heard my muttered complaint, Holmes paid attention to it, merely urging the pony to m better speed.

Before I had time to sort my impressions of disconcerting afternoon into some semblanc order, Holmes had steered the trap off the into a small clearing and was even now hur towards the shore of the loch just visible th the autumn foliage.

"Come along, Watson, there's a good We have an appointment with a monster."

By the time I had disentangled mysel the trap and picked my way through th bracken, I found Holmes in an attitude I l well. He was spread-eagled on the ban oblivious of the wet ground or the

33

chill in the air, examining the lower bark of a nearby tree with a large round magnifying glass.

I was about to say—"*What* monster?" but I knew it to be pointless. He would explain to me in his own good time and not a moment before. Having apparently satisfied himself that the possibilities of the tree trunk had been exhausted and laying something he had carefully removed from the bark with tweezers on his folded handkerchief, he proceeded to crouch further along the bank, murmuring under his breath, as if he were keeping up a conversation with himself. At one point he traced a finger along the ʳround, then put it to his lips. Finally, he sprang) his feet and walked in my direction.

"For heaven's sake, Holmes," I expostulated. What are we doing in this dismal spot? And what) you mean about the monster?"

"Where is the poet in your soul, my dear llow?" he replied, looking more cheerful than I ɪd seen him all day. " 'I come from haunts of ot and hern . . . and monsters.' Tennyson . . . Or ɔstly. This, Watson, is the nesting ground—or rhaps I should say 'resting ground' of the Loch ɪss Monster. Here . . ." And he indicated with boot a deep, even groove in the bank that had ɔosed a quantity of bare mud—"is where it ered the water and there . . ." pointing to the ɛ that had absorbed him—"it was tethered . . ."

34

"You mean, somebody managed to tie the monster up?" It came out sounding absurd but the idea seemed so ludicrous.

"Just so, Watson, just so. By the depth of the groove in the bank, I should estimate a length of some twenty feet, a displacement of just over a ton—not counting, of course, the two men in its belly."

I wondered if I could believe my ears. Perhaps all this talk of *Alice in Wonderland* had affected my friend's brain. Seeing the expression on my face, Holmes finally took pity on me.

"Forgive me, Watson, but your honest reaction to events is more necessary to me than you can ever know. You curb my excesses and bring me back to basics. Take a look at this . . ."

He unfolded the handkerchief and lying on it I saw two small fragments of wire. "These, Watson, are torn from a high tension wire cable capable of taking considerable strain. The fact that the cable has frayed at all suggests it was restraining something of a significant mass. Restraining—or mooring. Had that object been a living creature, I think we could safely expect the groove it made entering the water to show some signs of irregularity, suggestive of whatever appendages it uses to manoeuvre through the water. Instead, the groove is perfectly smooth . . ."

"Like the hull of a ship?"

"In a nutshell—a ship or, more specifically, a

submersible, holding, I would guess, two men—one to steer and one to manipulate the super-structure Mr. Moxton's guests saw as the 'monster'. You will no doubt recall, Watson, that our French friends launched a torpedo boat, the *Gymnote* some ten years ago. Since then I am informed that experiments have been undertaken to make such machines both lighter and more flexible. And what with the contribution of Herr Rudolf Diesel . . ."

He indicated the black liquid on his finger.

"A lightweight fuel oil which will make the steam engine archaic. And there you have Moxton's Monster."

"A fraud," I cried indignantly, "a damned fraud! And yet tomorrow he's going to tell the world the monster exists and he'll have witnesses to back up his story. It's incredible!"

"I'm afraid that's the one thing it won't be, Watson. Moxton's theory of the nature of truth is becoming all too credible. You read about a thing—therefore it is. Especially if there's a large picture to go with it. And I think we may safely deduce that tomorrow's *Clarion* will carry precisely such a photograph. In fact, I'd be prepared to wager that front page was already set and waiting some time before we were witness to his little charade. If he sincerely believes that a word can mean what he chooses it to mean and if Confucius is correct in his assumption that a picture is worth a *thousand* words . . . I leave the mathematics to you."

"You mean that the perception is as good as the truth?"

"Better, Watson, better. Particularly if people are given the perception they would like to see. No, I'm afraid that in the future people like our friend—with the aid of sufficient funds and the available technology—will be able to provide the so-called 'people' with a version of the world they would prefer to live in. And if the uncomfortable reality should occasionally leak through, well . . . twenty-four hours and another headline will conveniently cover it up again."

"But Holmes, if you're even remotely right, this is insupportable. We must do something—but what?"

"I'm very much afraid, old friend, that we must revisit Reichenbach and finish the job I had foolishly assumed was over seven years ago."

I must have looked rather like one of the fish I had been singularly unsuccessful in catching earlier but Holmes was kind enough to make no mention of my open mouthed stare. Instead, as he swung himself up into the driver's seat and helped me up beside him, he merely added in a conversational tone.

"I had assumed you realised that Moxton is our friend Moriarty? Now, I believe I promised you a decent dinner?"

CHAPTER THREE

M oriarty?"
    "Yes, Watson—Moriarty. If you repeat his name one more time in that tone of voice it will make a round twenty times of asking."

"But the world knows that Moriarty died at the Reichenbach Falls . . ."

"Just as the world knew I died at the Reichenbach Falls—except that now it knows that I didn't And if you're not going to eat that last piece of Stilton, you might edge it this way. The fresh air seems to have given me quite an appetite."

Abstractedly I did as he asked. "But how did you spot him, Holmes?"

Now my friend grew serious at last. "I admit, Watson, I have had the advantage of you. I sensed his presence, just as I did all those years ago. Lots of little things began to add up again—a case of arson here, a murder or an industrial dispute there . . . all the individual threads admittedly tenuous but slowly coming together to weave a pattern, a web of disruption and evil. At first I could not believe it—perhaps because I did not want to— but then I was forced to face the fact that I had seen such a pattern before and only one man was capable of weaving it. One Napoleon of

Crime is perhaps inevitable in a lifetime—but two?

"Then increasingly, the face of the spider in the middle of the web began to clear. The name of John Moxton began to crop up too often for either comfort or coincidence. Moxton or one of his associates. You noticed 'Professor James' this afternoon?"

"Fellow with the box of tricks? Certainly. Why?"

" 'Professor James' is no more a professor than you are, Watson. He used to go by the name of Kurt Krober. At least he did when he was one of Moriarty's henchmen. And if those wires were connected to anything, I'll eat Lestrade's bowler hat.

"Which reminds me." He took out a folded paper from an inside pocket. "This cable came from Lestrade while we were out enjoying ourselves. I asked him to contact my old friend, Wilson Hargreave of the New York Police Bureau to find out all that is known about the mysterious Mr. Moxton. Let's see what he has to say . . ."

He unfolded the several sheets and scanned them quickly. "Ah, most interesting. Let me see . . . John Moxton, born New York City, June 1839 . . . etc. . . . etc. . . . entered family publishing business . . . takes over in 1887 . . . quite a modest little enterprise by the look of it and Moxton appears to do little to change its fortunes . . . ah, here we are, Watson. 1893 Moxton apparently suffers a complete breakdown quite unanticipated by his colleagues and friends. The man is a widower with only one sister living . . ."

"Alicia's mother?"

"Quite so, Watson," Holmes shot me a thoughtful glance. "Miss Creighton's mother and herself a widow. Mother and daughter had not seen Moxton for many years, since they lived in Europe. Moxton, therefore, had, in effect, no close family. He was apparently whisked away to a sanatorium and kept in total seclusion under the care of his personal physician, Julius Minton . . ."

Holmes turned the page. "A year later he returns to New York fully recovered. His co-workers are impressed by the new energy he now brings to his work. Many of them describe him as 'a new man'. From that point the business takes off dramatically. Moxton apparently turns into a veritable tycoon, arranging financial deals that transform this rather sleepy little publishing house into a force to be reckoned with . . ." He skimmed the rest of the report. "And the rest, as our American friends are fond of saying, is history. Exit John Moxton. Enter the new John Moxton . . ."

"But what makes you so sure he's Moriarty, Holmes? Admittedly I only caught a glimpse of him at Reichenbach but I was left with an impression of a tall thin man, almost cadaverous . . ."

"Much easier for a thin man to become a fat

one, Watson, than for a naturally heavy man to lose weight—as I think you will agree?"

I hastened to change the subject. Mrs. Hudson's good plain cooking was taking its toll on my waist line and I suddenly realised that when I had met Miss Creighton earlier I was conscious of holding in my stomach. Such is male vanity! Fortunately Holmes was in no mood to be diverted from the trail. "And, of course, a clever tailor can add immeasurably to the desired effect."

"But the face? The man *looks* nothing like Moriarty."

"Yes, indeed, the face . . ."

Holmes pondered the question as he took out one of his favourite pipes and filled it with some foul-smelling concoction. Not to be outdone, I produced my own pipe and soon my Arcadia mixture was at least providing a protective cloud. "There are only two men in the world who presently have the skill to reconstruct a face with that degree of subtlety. Soon, I have no doubt, such cosmetic surgery will become a veritable industry and we shall all be able to change our appearance as often as we change our clothes. But today . . . ?

"I would have said Duchamps of Utrecht . . . particularly skilled with the eyes. You remember we ran across him a couple of years ago in the case of the politician, the lighthouse and the trained cormorant—and by the way, old fellow, when are you going to get around to writing that one up? It was not without its points of interest. Where was I? Ah, yes, Duchamps . . . I believe we can rule him out. I hear he is serving the pleasure of the Belgian authorities . . . which leaves us with Zuckerman of Boston . . . Yes, the nose has all the hallmarks of Zuckerman's work and, unless I miss my guess, we shall find that Moxton just happened to be taken to Zuckerman's clinic after his 'breakdown.'"

"So Moriarty becomes Moxton?"

"Moriarty becomes Moxton and brings all his considerable financial resources to bear using the real Moxton's publishing company as a base of operations. Let us not forget, Watson, that when his empire was supposedly broken up and scattered to the four winds, no one really knew precisely where he had secreted his ill-gotten gains. There were twenty known bank accounts apart from the Crédit Lyonnais and it is reasonable to believe these were only the tip of the iceberg. It would be a simple matter to channel them deviously back to the new centre of the web."

"But what about Alicia—Miss Creighton?"

"That, admittedly, was something Moriarty had not bargained for. The mother's will left the girl in her brother's charge and the new Moxton could hardly renege on the arrangement without drawing unnecessary attention to himself. *Ergo*, she becomes his ward and is now living under circumstances of some considerable danger, if she did but know it."

I remembered the look on that lovely face and knew instinctively that Alicia Creighton had more than a suspicion that something was amiss. Holmes was still musing on the reincarnated Moriarty.

"You know, Watson, even the cleverest criminals—and heaven knows, Moriarty is the cleverest of them all—give themselves away by the tiniest things, the merest trifles. And my method, as you know better than anyone, is based on the observance of trifles . . ."

"What trifle did I overlook in this case?" I asked, knowing that it was my expected response.

"Personal vanity. The crisis of identity, even when one is seeking to camouflage that identity. The criminal who changes his name will, more often than not and quite by instinct, craft a new name with the same initials, J.M. James Moriarty becomes John Moxton—even for a time Julius Minton. Another habit that is hard to shake off is the nervous mannerism. We all have them and are usually totally unaware of their existence. You, for example, chew the end of your moustache when you are concentrating—you are doing it this very moment."

Naturally, I stopped immediately and gave the offending decoration a quick brush with the back of my hand.

". . . Moriarty has the habit of pinching the bridge of his nose and it was perfectly clear to me that Moxton was finding it difficult to adjust to the more fleshy protuberance the surgeon's knife had left him with." He found this so amusing I did not have the heart to tell him that he had precisely the same nervous habit as his old rival.

"But had I been in any doubt—which by that time I most certainly was not—his handshake confirmed it. It went against the grain to offer him my hand, I can tell you, Watson, but it served its purpose. Moriarty had a protuberance on the wrist bone of his right hand. So, by an amazing coincidence, does Moxton. QED."

"So what's his little game, Holmes?" I asked.

"Money, of course, but mainly power. The sight of other people running around like ants, while he decides which to tread on and which to spare. Power through chaos. Chaos is his minion. Words are his new weapons. I very much fear, Watson, that we are fast approaching a point where many of the old rules are stretched to breaking point and the cynical bid fair to inherit the earth. In such a context a man like Moriarty naturally thrives. There is a strain of pure evil in his blood which his extraordinary mind raises to the power of—well, I would hesitate to calculate."

"What do we do now, Holmes?" I asked the

question that had been tormenting me throughout his explanation. "Call in Scotland Yard? Unmask him?"

"Nothing so straightforward, I'm afraid, old fellow. At this moment the man has committed no crime. To prove that he is not who he says he is would involve endless complications, starting with a defensive wall of lawyers a mile deep—not to mention alerting the man, when we need him, if not off his guard, then at least so overconfident that he believes himself to be impregnable.

"The game is afoot, Watson, and will not be over until we have led this Napoleon to his own Waterloo. For the time being we need do nothing but wait. I have never been surer than I am of the fact that Moriarty will come to me. A game of this kind—whatever game that turns out to be—is not worth the candle to him unless he beats me into the bargain. He wants revenge, Watson, revenge for the ignominy of Reichenbach, as he sees it. He let me catch his scent, I'm sure of it, for he knows I will follow the trail."

He puffed for a moment in silence, then said, almost to himself—"The *yin* and the *yang*—the twin principles of the ancient Chinese universe. The Chinese believed that the one could not exist without the other. Perhaps the Professor and I are like that. We shall see . . .

"And now, my dear chap, you've had the

dinner I promised you and who knows when we may have this breathing space again? Time to turn in, I think. We really do have a train first thing in the morning . . ."

CHAPTER FOUR

I came down to breakfast in Baker Street a couple of mornings later to find Holmes crouched on the floor amidst a heap of newspaper cuttings that he was moving around like chessmen, trying one first in one position, then another, before finally committing himself. The fact that he was wearing his mouse-coloured dressing gown as well as smoking his favourite old black pipe was enough to alert me to the fact that serious work was in progress.

Coughing discreetly to announce my presence—as well as to disperse the claustrophobic fog sufficiently to reach the breakfast table in comparative safety—I picked up my own paper and was relieved to see that it appeared to be intact. It would not have been the first time that the *Daily Chronicle*, by which I set such store, had been an early morning sacrifice to Holmes's insatiable need to clip and file. "I see we have a three pipe problem on our hands," I remarked, "and that you are at present at the third pipe stage?"

"Excellent, Watson. Your powers of deduction must never be underestimated, I see. I assume you made a mental note of the number of piles of plugs and dottle accumulated on the mantelpiece before retiring for the night. Then, having decided that it would be impolitic to sweep a few into the embers of the fire, in case I had made my own calculations, reluctantly decided to endure my matutinal conflagration for the sake of domestic peace?"

"Something of the sort," I muttered grudgingly, flicking through the paper, so as not to give him the satisfaction of total submission. "I suppose I left incriminating fingerprints on the mantelpiece?"

"Not to my knowledge, old fellow. I simply happened to be observing you through the crack in my bedroom door." Which thought appeared to amuse him immoderately. Sometimes the man is positively childish. All of which was immediately forgotten when I came to study the front page properly.

"Have you seen this, Holmes?" I cried. "Absolutely appalling state of affairs!" I held out the paper.

"Almost certainly not," my friend replied, still absorbed by his jigsaw of cuttings. "As you know perfectly well, I read little beyond the crime news and the agony columns. There is enough disaster, scandal and calumny reported there to fill several normal lifetimes. What social peccadillo in particular has caught your eye? Some lady turned away from the Café Royal for smoking

Turkish cigarettes? Some major from the shires blackballed for wearing the wrong coloured socks in the card room?"

"You may joke," I said, with what I hoped was a chilly dignity, "but the sight of the seat of government infested with vermin is hardly likely to raise our status in the eyes of the rest of the world. It says here . . ." And I began to read from the paper . . .

"OF MICE AND MEN . . . AND RABBITS!

House of Commons Chaos.

Parliamentary business was disrupted for several hours yesterday when the lower chamber was suddenly overrun with several dozen white rabbits. The animals appear to have been introduced through the heating vents and proceeded to run amok. It was several hours before the last of them was caught and removed and the Speaker could restore order to the proceedings. The spectacle of senior—and in many cases, nationally prominent—politicians standing on their benches to avoid contact with the rabbits, many of whom (the rabbits, that is) proved to be incontinent due to the excitement of the occasion, was more reminiscent of a music hall farce than the usual dignified deliberations conducted in the hallowed premises. As one newly elected (Independent) MP confided to this reporter on condition of anonymity: 'It certainly raised the interest level of a rather boring debate.

We should do this more often.' The police are pursuing their enquiries . . . etc., etc."

The paper was unceremoniously snatched out of my hands and Holmes was striding up and down the room devouring the story.

"Rabbits, rabbits . . . white rabbits. Of course . . ."

"Of course, what?" I asked testily.

"*Alice*, of course. Here, Watson, look at this . . ." He riffled through the cuttings on the floor until he found what he was looking for, a small piece of paper roughly torn around the edges. He threw it on the table in front of me, narrowly missing a soaking in my cup of tea.

"This was in this morning's *Daily Gazette*."

It was a typical item from the daily agony column. There was a single line of type that said . . .

"OH MY EARS AND WHISKERS, HOW LATE IT'S GETTING!"

. . . and beneath it a freehand drawing that looked like a smile. Below the drawing it was signed—"The Cat."

The whole thing was quite incomprehensible to me. I handed the cutting back to Holmes with an interrogative glance.

"It looked good-natured, she thought: still it had very long claws and a great many teeth, so she felt that it ought to be treated with respect."

He was talking to the piece of paper more than to me.

"The Cat, Watson. The Cheshire Cat in *Alice*. Don't you see—it's started. This is Moriarty throwing down the gauntlet. His strategy—whatever it is—is moving into high gear and he's challenging me to try and stop him. He knows that I am the only man in London who is likely to connect a communication like this with the actual event. Don't you remember the conversation about *Alice* up at Loch Ness? He's identifying himself."

"But what on earth has this to do with yesterday's debacle?"

"In *Alice* one of the characters is the White Rabbit and when Alice meets the Rabbit, she hears it say just those words. Moriarty wants me to know that it was he who organised what you call 'yesterday's debacle' in the House and he's also warning me that it's getting late. Though late for what we have still to determine . . .

"The exercise on which I was engaged when you entered was my attempt to piece together a pattern of Moriarty's recent activities and, as you can see, it is not without complexity." He indicated with a casual movement of his foot a series of rough circles, one within the other, moving outwards like ripples on the surface of a pond. "Each of these incidents apparently unrelated but, in reality, deviously interconnected.

Each of them contributing to a general picture of administrative corruption or governmental incompetence—or both—and most with a probability of financial gain for someone whose name I think we know by now."

"So you already have our friend by the heels?"

"No, Watson. In all of these cases the trail ends in a cul-de-sac long before it can be traced to Moriarty. I have Lestrade looking into a handful of them but, candidly, old fellow, I am not optimistic about the outcome. Frankly, for the moment our best hope is that his obsession with our personal vendetta may lead him to become careless. That's probably Lestrade at the door now."

We had both heard the insistent clang of the front door bell and Mrs. Hudson's footsteps hurrying to answer it. "Perhaps you'll be good enough to perform the usual courtesies while I change into more suitable attire. We must not let the law find us less than prepared to greet them. Particularly after yesterday's debacle. I would have given a great deal to have seen old . . ." And here he named an eminent Cabinet Minister— "chased by a white rabbit . . ."

Scooping the cuttings into a loose bundle, he dropped them casually behind his armchair, where Mrs. Hudson would sooner or later find them and agonise over whether or not to attempt to tidy them. He then hurried into his bedroom and shut the door firmly behind him—just as there was a knock on the door that led to the stairs.

"Come in, Lestrade," I called out, thinking to surprise him with my powers of deduction. Instead, it was the head of our worthy house-keeper, Mrs. Hudson that appeared around the edge of the door.

"It isn't Inspector Lestrade, Doctor Watson. It's . . ."

"It's Mycroft," I heard a deep voice say and the next thing I knew the massive figure of Holmes's elder brother was filling the portals of our sitting room.

"Good morning, Doctor, forgive me for bearding you in your den but I think you know I would not venture so far forth so early in the day—or at any time, come to that—were the occasion not of some significance?"

And indeed, I did know that the virtual giant now lowering himself carefully into Holmes's chair—having first fastidiously brushed it with the pristine white handkerchief he took from his pocket—was not in the habit of venturing far from the musty confines of the Diogenes Club in Pall Mall, if he could possibly help it. Holmes was always joking that the club, of which his brother was a founder member, was the "club for the unclubable" and one of London's best kept secrets. Yet from his regular armchair imme-diately to the left of the fireplace Mycroft

Holmes kept a hooded beady eye on the country's affairs. Although without any official status that one was aware of, he appeared to be the junction of all governmental paths or, as Holmes once described him, "the central exchange, the clearing house" of problems and events. "Watson, if only my brother would bestir himself, he would demonstrate the greatest deductive brain the world has yet seen. His powers far exceed my own."

This, then was the man sitting opposite me, perfectly relaxed in his chair, despite the weighty matter, whatever it might be, that had winkled him out of his preferred *modus vivendi*. As we sat there, with me making small talk, I reflected that this was only the third time in my long association with Holmes that I had met his brother. There had been—let me see—the affair of *The Greek Interpreter* and, only two or three years earlier, the infinitely more fraught case of *The Bruce-Partington Plans*, where the nation's very security had been involved.

Nor could I forget—though I had long since forgiven—the fact that it had been Mycroft and not I in whom my friend had confided the truth during the "Grand Hiatus". If ever two brothers qualified for the term "distant relations", it was these two. Still, there was undoubtedly something telepathic between them that more than compensated for the lack of corporeal contact.

This was demonstrated admirably to me as Holmes emerged from his bedroom.

"Good heavens, Mycroft here? The planet has left its orbit . . ."

"Am I correct in my deduction, Sherlock?" Mycroft did not waste time with the usual fraternal niceties.

"As ever," replied my friend.

"Loch Ness?"

"And White Rabbits."

"A bad business."

"The worst possible."

It was like watching two people play verbal chess. The moves were stripped down to the bone. Then, as though they became aware of the presence of a third person in the room who must be allowed into the game . . .

"Our own sources have been receiving the same signals for several months," said Mycroft, and I noticed that, seated on opposite sides of the empty fireplace, the two brothers had instinctively adopted the identical pose. Sitting back in their chairs, their fingers steepled in front of their faces, each was gazing into the middle distance without ever making eye contact with the other. They looked for all the world like a pair of mismatched bookends. I had no need to ask who "our" referred to but I couldn't refrain from asking—"But what are 'you' going to do about it? Nobody knows better than we what

Moriarty is capable of. Just what devilish plot do you believe he is hatching? Is he trying to bring down the Government—or what?"

Two pairs of piercing eyes turned my way and I was glad that their expression was friendly, for I should not have cared to be the object of hostile scrutiny. It was Mycroft who spoke.

"That, my dear Doctor, is the least of his ambitions, I fear. For some time now—and particularly at the last election—we have received reports of certain—shall I say, less 'orthodox' candidates receiving considerable financial support from anonymous sources. Many of them are now Members of Parliament, some as 'Independents', others creating friction on the back benches of the two main parties . . ."

"Steel," I interrupted, "that Steel fellow. Shifty looking customer. I said to Holmes."

"Just so, Doctor. Creighton Steel has emerged as their natural focus in the House and the country at large—helped immensely, I might add by the visibility given to his every utterance by John Moxton's *Clarion*."

"It would appear, old fellow," Holmes picked up the thread, "that if it can be so arranged that public opinion can be so influenced as to believe that the country is ungovernable by the present conventional means, then an alternative and more disciplined force is waiting in the wings, ready and able to step in and do so."

"Britain Needs A Touch Of Steel?" I quoted.

"Precisely, Watson. The plot in a nutshell."

"But the British people will never fall for such a far-fetched scenario, surely?"

"Don't be too sure," Mycroft interposed. "The heady days of Empire and Britannia ruling the waves by apparent divine right are over—almost certainly never to return. Her Majesty is ageing and her European cubs are already straining at the leash—the Germans in particular.

"There is unrest around the Empire. War in South Africa seems to me to be inevitable within a year or so. The British people are not political animals but they have a sense of the way the wind of change is blowing and, whether they identify the source of their concern or not, they are beginning to find it blowing chill. And since solutions are infinitely more attractive to them than problems, it won't take them long to gravitate to someone who seems to offer an articulate and painless way out of the dilemma. Which is why, Sherlock . . ." and here he looked Holmes in the eye for the first time—"my Cabinet Lords and Masters have delegated me to enlist your help in the national good. Will you help us cut out this worm in the bud?"

My friend, I could see, was enjoying himself. Reaching across, he tapped Mycroft on the knee.

"First of all, my dear brother, I don't believe you *have* any 'Lords and Masters'. What's more, neither do you! In the second place—as I'm sure your sources have informed you—I have already committed myself to completing the task in which I so singularly failed at Reichenbach."

"Forgive me for being obtuse," I interjected, "but precisely how are a handful of rabbits, white, brown or spotted, likely to bring down the British Government?"

"In and of themselves, of course, they're not, Watson. That was merely Moriarty's private joke, designed to ensure he kept my attention. His true purpose is infinitely more sinister, I can promise you and I feel sure its expression is imminent.

"Moriarty has come upon two tools that can be turned to infinitely deadlier effect than any mechanical device the mind of man could dream up," Holmes continued. "Public opinion and propaganda. Neither of them new but by utilising the new technology the one can work on the other in a way never before possible. An event no longer needs to be true—it merely has to be *seen* to be so. The perception becomes the truth. I tell you, Watson, the day will come when he who has the biggest lie and the deepest pockets will have the means to turn the world on his axis. It is a grave commentary on the gullibility of human nature and the power of organised rumour. But that is precisely what our friend is about to assay."

"You really mean one determined man can do that?"

"In fact and fiction men with sufficient nerve have been doing just that down the centuries—all they lacked were the means of sufficient influence," Mycroft interceded. "Dickens, you will recall, had his Mr. Merdle and Trollope his Augustus Melmotte. Two more M's. Swindlers and charlatans operating at the highest levels of society and leading that society by the nose until they were finally unmasked and ended up taking their own lives. I very much doubt that we can expect Moriarty to be quite so fictionally tidy."

"I find it hard to believe that the British people will swallow this," I said with more bravado than I truly felt. Sherlock and Mycroft's logic had all too much of the ring of truth about it for me to feel as sure of my ground as I would have dearly liked.

Holmes, as ever, sensed my distress at the thought of the world I knew being turned upside down.

"We must take change and use it, old friend, or face the certainty that there are those who will eagerly use it for their own ends and invariably to our disadvantage. All of us cling to what we know or think we know. We may well grumble but we respect the need for a hierarchy, so that we know our place. People—and the British people more than most—need to have an underlying respect for those who lead them. And this is the fiendishly clever part of Moriarty's plot. He realises full well that they will find it hard to sustain that respect when faced with the spectacle of leaders who seem unable to avoid the banana skins of life. What we are witnessing, however, is what I fear will prove to be something of a prologue to Moriarty's real theme—a grim joke, no more."

"And a brief one, too, I fancy," Mycroft completed the thought. As he spoke, he pulled a large turnip watch from his waistcoat pocket. "And talking of time, I must be on my way. In my unofficial 'official' capacity I have been asked to attend a function that may interest you both. There is to be an unveiling of a new bust of the Foreign Secretary at Madame Tussaud's this morning."

"Ah, a waxwork of a waxwork?" I snorted, not being enamoured of the gentleman in question. Mycroft turned his massive head in my direction.

"Let us say that Her Majesty's front bench has reverberated with greater animation than that often demonstrated by its present incumbent. And one might, indeed, wonder why an institution as populist as Madame Tussaud's should choose the Right Honourable Member as a subject of special interest, were it not for one incidental factor . . ."

In a mere mortal I would have sworn that the eye had a distinct gleam in it. And here he took out a gilt-edged card from a capacious inside pocket and read aloud: "Great Britons. A Commemorative Series of Statues Commemorating Our Nation's Leaders." He paused for a beat and the effect was suitably dramatic. When these two brothers took to their respective chosen occupations the stage lost the peers of Irving and Tree.

"Sponsored by The John Moxton Trust and the *Clarion* . . ."

Holmes leaped to his feet, suddenly full of purpose. "Come along, Watson," he cried, as though I were the habitual laggard. "Stir yourself. I have a distinct feeling that Act Two is about to begin . . . !"

CHAPTER FIVE

I strongly doubt that the vast majority of London's teeming thousands who pass its doors daily think of Madame Tussaud's Waxworks as anything but an intrinsic part of the local scene. If they ever paused to wonder at the rather unusual name, they have long since stopped doing so. For them it is as much a part of childhood as one of the parks.

For Holmes and myself it was something we passed regularly to and fro—sometimes several times a day, situated as it is on Marylebone Road, a mere stone's throw from Baker Street.

Founded at the very dawn of the century by a formidable Swiss lady, Madame Marie Grosholtz, who had herself trained in Paris, it had grown into a peculiarly British institution, though, for the life of me, I have never been able to appreciate its charm. To see an inanimate approximation of those who dominated their times usually by their sheer life force rather than their looks seems to me a contradiction in terms. But presumably, as Holmes so often reminds me, I fail to move with those times.

The fact remains that, on all the occasions I was dragged through the place as a child, I never saw anything half as lifelike as that Oscar

Meunier bust of himself Holmes had made to deceive Moriarty's lieutenant, Colonel Sebastian Moran, when "the second most dangerous man in London" was bent on revenging his supposedly dead master. As I recall, I wrote that episode up under the title of *The Empty House* and, for once, managed to receive my friend's tacit approval for one of my narratives.

Perhaps—I thought as Mycroft's carriage made the short journey from our lodgings to the wax emporium—there might be some small coincidence here. Moriarty . . . wax . . . Holmes . . . ? But then, reading tea leaves has never been my cup of tea, so to speak.

The carriage pulled up at the entrance to the establishment and already it was clear that this was no ordinary day. For one thing the crowds lining the entrance were several deep and obviously there to watch those who came in and out, rather than pay their money to go inside. A cordon of uniformed police were holding them back to let the genuine visitors through and the usual good-natured banter was being exchanged. As will often happen, the crowd had picked on one unfortunate subject for their so-called humour. He was standing with his back to us as we prepared to alight, wearing a long non-descript coat and a bowler hat that had seen better days.

"Coo, they've left one of the dummies outside,"

cried one anonymous wag from the back of the crowd.

"Nah, I saw 'im breathe," a woman's voice shouted.

"Go on, stick a pin in 'im!"

"Now, see here, my good woman," the bowler hatted man said, turning to face the crowd and it was then that I recognised our old friend, Inspector Lestrade of Scotland Yard. Small and rather ferrety of feature, Lestrade's path and ours had crossed many a time and oft. The relationship was always inclined to be touchy but over the years a healthy mutual respect had developed and Holmes often referred to him as the "pick of a bad lot"—a term I doubt the Inspector would have appreciated as unqualified praise. The fact that he was here in person, however, was due testimony to the fact that the Yard was taking security seriously and this was confirmed for me a moment later by the glance he exchanged with Mycroft, as the latter lowered his bulk to terra firma.

"Morning, gentlemen," he said touching the brim of his hat to Mycroft and Holmes in turn then, giving me the benefit of the doubt, adding one more for good measure. In reply to Mycroft's raised left eyebrow, he added: "My men have the whole place sealed off tight as a drum. I think you could say everything's tickety-boo."

"You *could*—but I wish you wouldn't, Lestrade,"

said Holmes, looking at the Inspector quizically. "Her Majesty's English receives enough punishment in this day and age without your adding further to it. Perhaps you'll show us to where the ceremony is taking place?"

Soon we were walking through the spacious entrance hall that would normally have echoed with the "Oohs" and "Aahs" of excited visitors. This morning the whole place had been temporarily closed to the public, another evidence of the power of Moxton's pocket allied to the snobbery of class. Our esteemed Foreign Secretary clearly had no wish to brush his imperial robes against his humble servants and voters.

Several liveried attendants stepped forward to meet us but Lestrade self-importantly brushed them aside in a manner that was clearly meant to communicate who was running this particular show. Did Moxton take all these servants around in a pack, I wondered, or did he have a reservoir of them at each port of call?

Before I could resolve such a weighty question, we were ushered into a side gallery filled with a group of people that—if logic didn't dictate otherwise—I could have sworn were the very same ones I had last seen by the banks of Loch Ness. Surging forward to greet us was Moxton himself. Even though I now knew that I watching a persona being worn like a mask, I couldn't help being impressed by the sheer performance. The man could impersonate the Sphinx and carry it off. I found Gilbert's lines from *HMS Pinafore* going through my mind . . .

> For he might have been a Roosian,
> A French or Turk or Proosian,
> Or perhaps Itali-an.
> But in spite of all temptations
> To belong to other nations,
> He remains an Englishman.

I must have been humming it under my breath, because I received a strange look from Holmes and from Moxton—it seemed easier all round to keep thinking of him as Moxton on such an occasion—an amused: "If only, Doctor, if only. As it is we poor colonials—or, should I say ex-colonials?—must play the hand we are dealt. Don't you agree, Mr. Holmes?"

"Indubitably, my dear M—Moxton." Holmes seemed to stumble over the first syllable. "Though I believe in many games of chance—and Watson knows far more about these things than I—it is customary to discard when one has an inconvenient card and, of course, there is always the element of bluff . . ."

"As usual, Mr. Holmes, you are clearly better informed than you would wish others to believe. I don't think I would care to face you across the poker table. And now, gentlemen, shall we . . . ?"

I was about to remind Holmes that he had yet to introduce Mycroft to Moxton/Moriarty, when I noticed that his brother was nowhere in sight. Like many large men, he could when he chose be remarkably light on his feet. Interpreting my glance, Holmes indicated the door to the Entrance Hall and murmured—"Affairs of State, Watson—Affairs of State. Mycroft is no doubt meeting our Distinguished Visitor."

"Oh, no, Mr. Holmes," Lestrade interjected. "The Foreign Secretary arrived several minutes ago. He and his aides asked if they could just wander around for a few minutes before the ceremony. Apparently, Lord —— has a soft spot for this place. Seems he used to come here as a kiddie."

I saw my friend's brows crease in a small frown, which was gone as fast as it came. "A politician of considerable native instinct, it would seem, Lestrade. It must be pleasing to converse with a constituency of the mute . . . Hello, what's this?"

Without our really noticing, Moxton had moved to the dais in the centre of the gathering, where a shrouded figure stood waiting to be unveiled. He was now conferring with a group of Museum officials and looking at his watch in an obtrusive manner, making it clear to anyone watching—which included most of those present—that events were now running behind schedule. Now he dispatched one of the liveried minions, who ostentatiously hurried from the room.

"I must apologise for this slight delay, ladies and gentlemen." Moxton held up his hands to gain attention. "We seem to have temporarily mislaid our guest of honour." He received polite laughter for his pains. "He's probably detained in a one-sided conversation with one of Madame's house guests." More laughter, louder this time. The man was playing his audience with the finesse of an Irving and rather more humour. "I spent five minutes myself chatting to one of the attendants on the way in before I realised just why he was being so uncommunicative!"

Now they were positively eating out of his hand. I looked at Holmes and those sharp features were focused on Moxton in an expression that told me nothing would deter him from his purpose. In the middle of this apparently convivial gathering a chill ran down my back. This was a play we were both watching and taking part in, yet when the curtain came down I knew this whole business could have but one ending and that a tragic one. Once again, I feared for my friend.

"I think we might give our honourable guest a few moments more, ladies and gentlemen. I think we all know, do we not, how difficult it is for a politician to give up a captive audience?"

Was it my imagination or was there an odd

inflection somewhere in that last sentence that I couldn't quite place? The whole room was beginning to take on an unreal aspect with the guests laughing mindlessly, while in the wings, so to speak, another frozen audience stood silently watching like a gallery of ghosts. Was one any more real than the other?

"Today," Moxton continued, "we are gathered to honour the first of our 'Great Britons'. My little paper, the *Clarion*, considers it a privilege and a pleasure to be able to make this small gesture . . . ah, I do believe we have what we journalists call some late-breaking news of our honouree . . ."

I could now see that the flunkey had returned and was whispering urgently into Moxton's ear. If the press lord was surprised at what he heard, he hid it well. Turning back to his guests, he said: "Ladies and gentlemen, it appears that urgent business has necessitated Lord ——'s immediate return to the corridors of power."

There was a murmur of surprise and some irritation that spread around the group but, Moxton soon quelled it. "Yes, I'm just as disappointed as you folks—but I guess that's why we're honouring this man . . . because he puts this country first."

He paused to acknowledge a scattering of applause. "So, because I know your calendars are all as full as mine—and almost as full as his—I suggest we honour him *in absentio*. Lady Bullard, would you be so kind . . . ?"

A large and imposing lady, who looked to have launched many a mighty ship of state in her time, stepped forward to be handed a gilt rope by Moxton in lieu of a bottle of champagne. With an energy and directness that must have served her well in the shires, she gave the rope a sharp tug and with startling suddenness the cover dropped from the statue. There was a palpable silence as the room held its breath as one. There in full military regalia, complete with sash and Order of the Garter stood the effigy of Lord ——, complete in every detail except one. He had no head!

The room erupted in pandemonium, a mixture of shock and embarrassed amusement. Holmes, I noticed, having taken in the spectacle at a glance, was now staring at the doorway, where Mycroft was looming over a nervous young police constable. In answer to his barely raised forefinger, we pushed our way through the disconcerted crowd to his side. Without appearing to hasten his pace, he led his party towards a flight of stairs at the far side of the entrance hall. Over his shoulder I heard him say: "I'm afraid there have been certain developments."

It was then that a childhood memory came rushing back. Suddenly I knew where Mycroft was taking us.

"Isn't this the way to what used to be called the 'Separate Room'—the Chamber of Horrors?"

A few steps further and we were in another world. Even though the museum had been moved a few years back, this particular room had been lovingly re-created in all its pseudo-Gothic splendour. One moment we were in Victoria's London, listening to the sound of our own footsteps echoing on the marble floor of the hall as we walked through intermittent shafts of autumn sunlight. Behind us the excited chatter from the room we had just left, like birds disturbed in their nest. The next moment we had descended into Hell.

I imagine most of my readers can recall their first experience of entering this eerie setting and the *frisson* of self-induced fear the place manages to conjure up, despite the fact that one knows that everything here is made by the hand of man and sometimes not even artfully so. I have always found it was not so much the reality as the concept of evil that was truly frightening; the horrors live in one's mind. And perhaps, just as some places have a distinct and almost tangible "atmosphere", this one retained a distillation of the emotions generations of visitors had left here. All I know is that each time I visit the place, chastising myself mentally for repeating the stupidity, I find myself holding my breath a little to catch the slight unexpected noise and

71

wondering whether I had really seen something move out of the corner of my eye that shouldn't be able to move. Was Marat standing quite like that the last time I saw him? And surely the ominously named Vlad the Impaler . . . ?

Another vaguely familiar wax figure caught my eye, because for some strange reason it appeared to be wearing a placard around its neck. I was about to go over and examine it, when Mycroft interrupted my uncomfortable train of thought.

"Perhaps you would care to inform our colleagues of this morning's unfortunate happenings, Lestrade?" At which point another of the waxworks I had been trying in vain to identify suddenly came to life. I inwardly cursed the man for raising my pulse rate several notches. The Inspector was clearly discomfited. Taking off his bowler and mopping his forehead with a none-too-clean bandana, he managed to avoid everyone's gaze.

"Well," he said, "it seems that the Foreign Secretary and his assistants were wandering around, like, and he decides he must pay a visit to the Chamber for old times' sake. Apparently, the place was a favourite of his from when he was a young lad . . ."

"Yes, yes," Holmes interrupted. "Get to the point, Lestrade."

Lestrade looked a little piqued to have his narrative flow interrupted but continued . . .

"Well, when they get down here, they thought they heard a noise in the corner. The next thing they knew, the two young chaps had been set upon, bound, gagged and left behind one of the exhibits. It was all over so quick, they couldn't see who attacked them and all they could hear was their boss putting up a struggle. After that, it went very quiet. The next thing they knew was when my lads came in with Mr. Mycroft here and found them. And that's the long and short of it."

"But the Foreign Secretary?" I could have shaken the man until his teeth rattled. "What happened to the Foreign Secretary?"

"Over here, Watson."

It was Holmes. Impatient with Lestrade's rambling discourse, he had made for the far end of the gallery, where two rather self-conscious constables were standing guard and doing their best to ignore one of the most bizarre spectacles I can remember seeing. A somewhat lurid replica of the Tower of London stood as the backcloth. In the foreground was the gigantic figure of the Executioner. Masked and stripped to the waist, he was exercising his exaggerated musculature by raising his double-edged axe on high. At his feet, arms bound behind his back and his head on the block, was a figure clad in full military regalia.

It took a second glance to ascertain that this was not just another wax dummy, even though its eyes were closed and it lay there quite motion-less. Those distinctive patrician features were all too familiar from newspaper photographs and caricatures. It was the Foreign Secretary with his neck on the block.

By this time Holmes was bending over him and Mycroft and the others had arrived. "Your department, Watson, I think. I don't believe he's come to any real harm. A touch of chloroform, I fancy, nothing more."

As I knelt to take his place and conduct a cursory examination, he added thoughtfully: "Except, of course, for one thing which is not without significance. It is not given to many of us to see ourselves face to face." With that he rose to his feet and for the first time we could all see the object his body had been shielding.

When Lord —— regained consciousness, he would find himself communing with himself. Literally eyeball to eyeball with the sleeping peer was the disembodied head of his own wax effigy.

CHAPTER SIX

Almost apologetically, it seemed to me, Mycroft fixed his gaze on the recumbent Foreign Secretary.

"I thought it as well, Sherlock, since his lordship was clearly sedated and feeling no pain, to leave the scene of the crime undisturbed. I know how you like to dig and delve."

And, to be sure, Holmes was already prowling around the prostrate Foreign Secretary. I could tell from his air of concentration that he had scarcely heard what his brother was saying.

It was Lestrade who was providing the background noise, talking as much to himself as anyone else. "Lummy, that's two in a row, what with the rabbits and this. A proper lot of fools we're going to look. I don't know what the Commissioner's going to say."

"He's not going to say anything," Mycroft answered tartly, "for the simple reason that he isn't going to *know* anything about it until I say so."

"I'm afraid it won't be that easy, my dear Mycroft," said Holmes straightening up and rejoining us, as he sifted through something in the palm of one hand with the forefinger of the other. "I think you will find that the news—like

Puck—has thrown a girdle round the earth . . . or at least as far as the room upstairs.

"The scuff marks on the floor clearly indicate a struggle between three men, two of whom overpower and drag the third—milord here—to his present ignominious position. All of this watched by another man who stood just here . . ." and he indicated the spot with the toe of his shoe—"and smoked a cigar for approximately three and a half minutes, almost certainly of the type now being generously offered to the gentlemen guests by our host. Unless I'm mistaken, this ash is of American origin, probably a blend of Havana and Virginia leaf. You might remember I once wrote a trifling monograph on the subject, Watson?"

"*Upon the Distinction Between the Ashes of Various Tobaccos*"—a study of 140 different varieties of pipe, cigar and cigarette tobacco—I could recite the piece by heart. "It would also be relatively easy to identify which of Moxton's servants were involved in the affray by a study of their shoes. No two leave identical marks. But that, I feel, would divert us from our proper purpose, Mycroft?"

Mycroft nodded almost imperceptibly. This was not a subject he cared to discuss in any but the most privileged company. At that moment the Foreign Secretary showed the first signs of stirring. At the same time I caught a glimpse of a corner of white paper on which he had obviously been lying. Stepping over, I quickly snatched it up.

"Good old Watson." Holmes gave me an approving nod. "Keeps his eye on the ball while the rest of us are staring around the outfield. What is Moriarty's arcane motto this time?"

The message was clearly from the same hand that had prepared the advertisement in this morning's paper. Once again the signature was the drawing of the grinning cat's face and this time the wording ran . . .

"HE'S MURDERING THE TIME! OFF WITH HIS HEAD!"

Silently I passed the note to Holmes who perused it carefully with Mycroft looking over his shoulder. "Of course, the Queen of Hearts never actually beheaded anyone," said Mycroft ruminatively.

"True," Holmes replied, "but then murder was not on the agenda today. By the way, gentlemen, I think his Lordship might be discreetly moved now for his greater comfort. The back door, I think." Several constables rushed to obey Lestrade's signalled instructions and shortly the three of us were alone once more.

"No," Holmes went on as he paced up and down with that familiar stride of a caged animal. There was something bizarre about the sight of

77

him walking in front of this silent gruesome audience, as if he were advising them to mend their ways. "Scandal and public concern remain the priority for the moment. Background noise, one might call it. Watson, you're the writer amongst us, wouldn't you take a small bet that tomorrow's *Clarion* will have something like . . .

'OUR HEADLESS GOVERNMENT!' or 'MINISTER LOSES HIS HEAD!'

. . . splashed all over its front page? And the others will feel they can't afford to be far behind, if they're to retain their circulation and what passes for journalistic credibility. The snowball appears to be gathering momentum . . ."

"Curiouser and curiouser," I found myself saying, to my surprise as much as theirs. This *Alice in Wonderland* business was catching!

As we left the Chamber the regular inhabitants seemed inanimately sorry to see us go. We may well have provided the most exciting *divertissement* to be seen there in a long time. After all, it can't be too often that the spectators provide the entertainment.

Just before we reached the door Holmes paused briefly to address one of the figures as one might greet an old friend.

"Poor old Charlie Peace. A virtuoso of the violin, Watson." He turned to me by way of explanation. "And an absolute Paganini on the one string fiddle. If only he'd stuck to plucking the strings instead of cutting throats, we might have played some interesting duets together. Which reminds me, I haven't taken the Stradivarius out of its case for days. You might jog my memory when we get home, old fellow?"

I made a firm resolve to do nothing of the sort.

It was almost certainly this piece of inappropriate tomfoolery on Holmes's part that prevented me from taking a second look at the figure that had half caught my eye as we entered that benighted dungeon. I had another half impression of a bearded medieval man with a plumed hat and holding something white and somehow out of keeping in his hand . . . and then Holmes and Mycroft between them had whisked me away. The presentation room crowds were thinning out as we reached the Entrance Hall, buzzing now more like busy bees than birds as they struggled into their coats and hats and made for the door. The general drift seemed to be that the whole episode was a disgrace and that "they"—whoever "they" were—should do something about it, the country was going to the dogs and so on. But under the trite expressions one could detect a sense of unease. These things were not supposed to happen—not here, not in England.

When we entered the room itself some of the immediate motivation became clearer. On the dais—standing next to the headless waxwork and making a perfect opportunity for several of the newspaper photographers to take his picture, which they were in the process of doing—stood Royston Steel. Whether he had been part of the crowd when we first entered or whether he had timed his entry more recently for maximum impact was not entirely clear. What was clear was that he was now milking the occasion for every last drop of righteous indignation.

And, no doubt about it, the man was a born orator. The Government was mentally and morally bankrupt . . . the Opposition was geriatric and traditionally infirm of purpose . . . Sodom and Gomorrah were just around the next corner and our enemies were massing to recreate Armageddon in England's green and pleasant land. It was time a few independent souls of like mind and will, etc., etc. It was arrant nonsense, of course, but it was mesmerising nonsense and one could see how he had gained his public reputation. Even Holmes, I could see, was reluctantly impressed with the display.

"The man only needs a burning bush and a few tablets of stone and we can all follow him to Kingdom come," he whispered.

"Which is precisely what the people of this country are going to do, Mr. Holmes."

It was Moxton at our elbow, contentedly puffing a large and expensive cigar.

"I hear on all sides that it is time for a change. By the way, Doctor, as a writer, may I ask your professional opinion of that for a slogan? 'Time For A Change!' Not bad, eh? One day a candidate is going to get elected with those same meaningless words."

This was the second time in a few minutes my literary credentials had been invoked in a distinctly patronising way. A snort of indignation was the only reply that seemed vaguely suitable.

Turning to Holmes, his tone changed. "My spies tell me our ubiquitous feline friend, the Cheshire Cat has been up to his tricks again? It was always one of my favourite characters in *Alice*. I always envied his—or was it her?—ability to appear and disappear at will. So convenient in today's world. The company bores you and— pouf!—all they're left with is the grin, 'which remained some time after the rest of it had gone', I seem to remember. Such a way with words, our Mr. Carroll. Or should I say Dodgson? Identity can be such a complex matter, don't you agree?"

Then, observing that Holmes was making movements to leave, he added—"Oh, Mr. Holmes, one more thing. I'm so grateful to you for reminding me of these past literary pleasures that I find they're becoming quite an obsession lately. So much so that I've decided to throw an *Alice* party at my London house tomorrow night. You must both come, now I insist. Everyone will dress as a character from the book. I feel sure you'll find the guest list interesting—what's the phrase I want? All the usual suspects. Or did I just think of that? Ah, well, like that other literary genius, Oscar Wilde, I shall no doubt persuade myself that I did."

"You may count on both of us, Mr. M-Moxton," said Holmes with again the slightest of pauses on the "M" and before I had an opportunity to make any excuse.

"Oh, and may I ask you one last favour? May I take one of your excellent cigars? I've been fascinated by them all evening."

Moxton immediately produced one from his cigar case but seemed to pause a moment before handing it to my friend.

"A cigar, Mr. Holmes? I was always told that you were a pipe man?"

"And I would never have put you down as a smoker at all. No, Watson here has been nagging me for some time about my filthy tobacco habits and I have determined to turn over a new leaf. And a new tobacco leaf seems as good a way to start as any. Good day . . ."

CHAPTER SEVEN

I awoke the next morning to a fusillade of sounds that my Army experience told me were undoubtedly gunshots. My first thought was that Moriarty had broken cover and decided on the ultimate direct approach. It was the work of a moment to snatch up my dressing gown and my service revolver, which was never far from my hand. Taking the steps two at a time—a risky business at my stage of life—I burst into the sitting room we shared . . . only to find Holmes hunched up deep in his armchair, a carton of Boxer cartridges in his lap, the detritus of the day's papers at his feet and a large hair trigger pistol pointed, or so it seemed, directly at my head.

"Good God, man," I sighed, for it was not the first time this little scene had occurred, "how often do I have to remind you that pistol practice is an open air pastime and, as far as I'm concerned, as far away and as late in the day as possible? To inscribe the sovereign's initials on our sitting room wall, while undoubtedly an enviable and patriotic talent, is equally one without redeeming social features. I would remind you that Mrs. Hudson has only just had that plaster repaired. What is she going to say?"

"Do you take me for a fool, Watson?" said Holmes, a suspicious twinkle in his eye. "Do you think that before embarking on this feat of derring-do I have not carefully ascertained that the good lady has embarked upon her morning visit to the shops, an excursion that will take her another . . ." and here he consulted his rather battered watch—"seven minutes? Now, be fair, old fellow, is that not my *chef d'oeuvre*?"

There on the wall, where once could be discerned the legend—"VR"—the bullet-pocks now read—"JM."

I sighed heavily and picked up what was left of my morning paper. "Any word from our feline friend?" I asked.

"Nothing under that particular imprimatur," my friend replied, "but then he doesn't need to boast this morning when the whole of Fleet Street is busy doing it for him. Even as I foretold you, my dear chap,"—and he scooped up a handful of assorted pages from the floor—"Listen to this . . .

'HEADLESS LEADERS WITH FEET OF CLAY?' The *Daily Gazette* . . . 'HOUSE OF PARLIAMENT—OR MUSIC HALL?'

"The *Daily News*. But leaving the sensationalists aside, the worrying content is what is starting to emerge in the serious press. Here's the *Telegraph* leader—'If the recent spate of events'—I think 'spate' is a little overstated but even so—'is any indication of the state of our national security, then perhaps we would be well advised to take greater heed of some of the more dramatic stories currently circulating in certain quarters. Only a short time ago the possibility of Nihilist or other organised extremists carrying out their activities on our shores would have seemed . . .'

"You can imagine the rest, Watson, knowing the *Telegraph*, as you do. Outraged Empire, 'Disgusted, Tunbridge Wells' and all that."

"So the devil is getting away with it?" I spluttered, annoyed as much as anything else with Holmes's *sang froid* and the fact that his observations on the futile fumings of certain of our fellow citizens were only too accurate.

"For the moment I'm afraid he is, old fellow. Here, let me pour you a fresh cup of tea before you choke on your toast. I told Mrs. Hudson you would probably need an extra spoonful of the Earl Grey to go with this morning's news. But to answer your question . . ." And now the levity was discarded with the crumpled papers. "We have little choice for the moment but to let Moriarty play his hand while we try and assess what cards he is really holding—or, indeed, what his true game is. Disruption, certainly, national instability. No need to ask what is meant by 'certain quarters.' The *Clarion* has been orchestrating for days these rumours of vague Nihilist plots, sightings of mysterious and notorious but conveniently unnamed European agents. They promote Dame Rumour and, if called into question, protest the sanctity of their 'sources' and the public's right to know. I very much fear, Watson, that—whatever the outcome of this little affair—Moriarty has unleashed a force far more sinister than any of his previous skulduggery and one which cannot be re-corked like a genie in a bottle."

"Perhaps we shall know more after this evening's affair," I suggested, more for something to say than with any real expectation. The picture Holmes had painted was black indeed: "Undoubtedly, old fellow. We are meant to be fed little tidbits to keep us interested. Moriarty is having a high old time at our expense but never forget for one moment that, while we are sniffing along his trail, he is constructing a guillotine over our heads rather more practical in its purpose than the one we saw yesterday in the good Madame's emporium."

As he spoke, once again I experienced the vague sense of having seen something significant there and, once again, it eluded me.

"He is being prodigal with his clues because he believes there is nothing we can do about them. It is up to us to prove him wrong and to lure him through arrogance into error. My sixth sense tells me that tonight may prove to be our friend's Ides, if not of March, then of—where are we now, Watson?"

"October," I said, verifying the date from the ravaged *Chronicle* I was holding. "October the Thirty-First. Halloween. Very appropriate!" Again that tiny mental bell rang insistently and I was on the verge of remembering why when . . .

Another bell sounded from the front door below.

Holmes raised an eyebrow: "Were we expecting anyone at this unearthly hour? I really am in no state to receive visitors." He pulled his dishevelled dressing gown tighter around him, as if in protest. "Watson, I wonder if you would be so good in Mrs. Hudson's absence . . . ?"

Muttering, "Not the only thing that's in no state to receive visitors," beneath my breath, I picked my way through the mess that Holmes had managed to make of the room we were supposed to share. Really, I had never known anyone who could create chaos out of domestic order with apparently so little effort. He had to be London's worst tenant—I sometimes wondered how that scalpel of a brain could tolerate such physical disarray. I could only assume it didn't see it. Or was it that my own all too short period as a married man had left me with certain indelible domestic standards?

Pondering such immensities, I trotted down the stairs and opened the door, fully expecting to see the ferrety features of Lestrade or one of his minions. Instead, I found myself facing the statuesque figure of—Alicia Creighton! Even with the long veil down and having only seen her the once, she was unmistakable. Although she could only have been of average height she had the comportment of the ladies one sees in the fashion plates.

Even now—when she was once again clearly tense, looking anxiously over her shoulder—her presence rendered me unable to think of a single thing to say. Instead, I simply stared at her, reflecting even as I did so that the woman must think me a deaf mute idiot. "Won't you come in, Miss Creighton?" I finally managed. She brushed past me, lifting her veil as she did so, and those blue-grey eyes drove whatever I might have said next clean out of my mind. Not since Irene Adler—*the* woman—had I encountered such a positive female presence and I remembered the complications that lady brought with her, though fortunately not to me . . . All this and I had yet to hear the lady utter a word.

Moments later we were in the sitting room and Miss Creighton was settling herself into my chair as I hastily did what I could to give the room a semblance of order. Then she spoke. The voice was low and perfectly pitched, almost a singer's voice and—miracle of miracles—it had a smile in it.

"If this is on my account, Doctor, please save yourself the trouble. You should see my room. I suspect a degree of untidiness is the natural state of bachelors of either sex!"

Before I could respond in kind I heard Holmes say—"How very true, Miss Creighton, but I sometimes think old Watson takes things a little too far. I frequently have to take him to task for desecrating the morning papers, for instance, before I have had the chance to catch up with the world's woes . . ."

"*I* desecrate . . . ?" I spluttered. At which an explosion of silent laughter shook Holmes's lean frame until it turned into a coughing fit, which made me feel justice had been served. A moment later we were all laughing and the ice was well and truly broken. The lady had obviously made two conquests.

"It's good to see you relax, Miss Creighton," said Holmes, suddenly serious, and I realised that the badinage had been a deliberate part of his stratagem.

"You have been under some considerable stress of late, I see."

Not for the first time was I aware of his almost hypnotic power of soothing a client when he had a mind to.

"I'm afraid that is all too obvious, is it not?" The eyes were lowered for a moment as she busied herself with removing her gloves. Then, as if she

89

had finally made up her mind to face whatever was concerning her, she looked directly at us. From the atmosphere in the room I could tell that Holmes was as aware as I of the underlying tension in the woman's presence.

"I would like you to call me Alicia, gentlemen, if that were possible? I need your help very much." For a moment the voice trembled slightly, then recovered its strength as she added simply, "There is no one else to turn to."

"Except your guardian . . . except that he is *not* your guardian," Holmes spoke so softly that his voice was hardly more than a whisper, yet it filled the silence of the room.

"But how do you know?" The colour left her cheeks, then came flooding back. The real Alicia Creighton came to life in front of our eyes, sitting forward eagerly in her chair. "It's true, you do see everything! Even my g— even he says so in his bitter way. I hear him talking of you many times to his friends when he does not think I can hear. He hates you for some reason, for something that happened long ago . . . but I think he fears you, too. You—how do you say?— obsess him. It is about that that I have come to see you, to warn you . . ."

Then, as if conscious that she was rushing her narrative, she composed herself. "But I should first go back a little. What do you know about me, Mr. Holmes?"

"Other than that you have been exposed to the French language and culture from an early age . . . have attended a finishing school, almost certainly in Geneva . . . have earned your living as a governess and are proud of your accomplishment as a seamstress, I can tell very little. Except, of course, that you are fond of dogs and of one in particular and that you have been worried of late. But the last you confirmed from your own lips."

Now the eyes took on a genuine sparkle of amusement, which temporarily banished the other feelings. "Mr. Holmes, everything I hear about you is true. You are a sorcerer!"

"Hardly that, Miss Creighton . . ."

"Please call me Alicia."

"Hardly that—Alicia. My little parlour trick—to which poor Watson has been witness more times than either of us cares to count—is based on pure observation and logic. The signs are there for anyone who has the wit to read them. Let me demonstrate.

"Although your vocabulary is perfect, you have a tendency to use a French construction with English words. This suggests that you have been taught to *think* in that *language*. An English person simply learning it would not do that. Then, the way you arrange your gloves, one across the other, as if your hands were folded in your lap is a piece of etiquette much favoured by ladies' finishing schools and one that lasts for life. But the way you entered the room and took your seat is taught exclusively by Madame Solange, a former dancer of no mean reputation whose Geneva establishment has a well deserved *cachet* . . ." Observing my amusement, he added for my benefit: "I had the pleasure of rendering the lady some small service during the course of my Swiss 'sabbatical' . . ."

"I see," I rejoined, "was that before or after you made your study of coal tar derivatives in Montpélier?"

But Holmes, once on the scent, was not to be deterred by would-be humorous trifles. He returned his undivided attention to Alicia Creighton.

"Despite that background, your hands bear evidence of light manual work. At first I thought a writer—there is evidence of ink on your index finger. But the principal signs point to the regular use of a needle—no, Watson . . ." He smiled, sensing my instinctive reaction—"not *the* needle. Hence I deduce a seamstress. That same right index finger indicates use of a thimble and the way your hands smooth the lace at your cuffs suggests you are pleased with your own handi-work. And since there are few alternatives for a young lady of a good family, a governess seemed the likely occupation."

"You're quite right, Mr. Holmes," she shook her head as I have seen so often when someone is exposed to Holmes's mental powers for the first time. "I do keep a journal religiously and I did earn my living as a governess after I left Madame Solange and before my guardian . . ." The mention of Moxton was clearly upsetting to her, so Holmes rapidly continued.

"The recent worry I detect from the bitten finger nails but it is equally clear that this is a recent and not a long-established habit. And as for the dog . . . it is plain that you are used to nursing a brown and white short haired terrier on your knee—probably a Jack Russell—something few ladies would permit in their finery unless they happened to be a genuine dog lover."

"Ah, yes, little Sonny, the housekeeper's dog. He has seen me through many a difficult hour, Mr. Holmes. It all seems so obvious when you explain it like that."

"Indeed it is obvious, if one trains oneself to look in the right direction. Watson will tell you that it has long been an axiom of mine that . . ."

". . . the little things are infinitely the most important," I completed for him.

Holmes caught my eye for half a beat. Then his smile encompassed us both.

"There will come a day, Alicia, when, if you have your Watson, you will no longer need your Holmes. And if I continue to indulge myself with explanations, my little bubble of reputation . . ."

"But that day will be a long time coming," I

hastened to add—and meant it most sincerely.

Alicia leaned forward in her chair. "In all of this I had almost forgotten that you already knew the very thing I had come to tell you. My 'guardian' . . ."

Holmes raised a hand to stop her. "I suggest you tell us about the events of the last few weeks in your own words, Alicia. Leave out no detail, no matter how small or apparently irrelevant."

"I'm afraid most of it comes down to what so many of my sex like to hide behind—a woman's feelings and much of it sounds so commonplace . . ."

"Ah, the good old 'commonplace'! Take my word for it, there is nothing so unnatural as the commonplace, eh, Watson? And as for feminine intuition, over the years I have come to the reluctant conclusion that a woman's 'impression' can often cut to the quick of a problem with greater precision that the mental scalpel of the analytical mind. Pray continue." And to encourage her to do so, he settled back with languid ease, his finger tips together and his eyes apparently fascinated by the ceiling.

Seemingly reassured by Holmes's words, our guest also settled back in her chair for the first time. Then she began to speak.

"You have to comprehend, Mr. Holmes—and you, too, Doctor . . ." the magnificent eyes flashed all too briefly in my direction—"although he was my mother's only brother, I never knew John Moxton well. I was a small child when my father died and my mother took me to Europe to start a new life. Oh, my uncle would write regularly and I have no doubt—even though my mother never referred to it—that he would send her small sums of money when he sensed things were difficult for us. In fact, I am virtually certain that it was he who somehow found the money to pay for my time with your friend, Madame Solange."

In anyone but Holmes I would have sworn I saw the suspicion of a blush. Alicia continued . . .

"Then one day the money stopped—or so I assumed. Certainly, I had to find myself a paid occupation as a governess in Paris. That was no problem for me but my mother's health was. I think she felt she should have been able to do more and that made matters worse. Then one day, through some friends from home who were passing through, we heard that the reason for all of this was that Uncle John had somehow been taken ill. Although she had not seen him for some time, my mother had always felt close to her brother and, frankly, Mr. Holmes, I think the news was the final straw. A few weeks later she was taken ill and died. The French doctors said it was pneumonia but the real reason I believe was that life had worn her out.

"For me life went on in the same old way. Naturally, I was lonely. The reason for being there was gone and really, I belonged nowhere and to nobody. When the lawyers told me that Uncle John was now recovered and was to be my guardian by my mother's wish, I was overjoyed. Three months ago I came to London to join him."

"And . . . ?"

"And he wasn't the same man. Oh, he *looked* the same as I remembered from all those years ago and from all the pictures—but something was very wrong. At first I put it down to the fact that I was very young when I'd last seen him but, then I began to notice that he got things wrong—family details, things like that."

Holmes looked at me reflectively. "The last thing our friend had expected was to have to deal at close quarters with a member of the immediate family. The best laid plans, eh, Watson? But pray continue. I shall not interrupt you further."

"Oh, he was clever, I must grant him that. He explained that his breakdown had affected his memory but that it would come back in time and he asked for my understanding. With anyone else I would have felt immediate sympathy but there was something about him that made me feel . . ." And here she shuddered at the memory, wrapping her arms around her shoulders as if a sudden chill had passed through the room. "For weeks I tried to reason with myself, then one day a week or so ago—I don't know what made me do it—I asked him if he recalled a particular incident involving him and my mother. I painted it in glowing detail and, anxious to please me—and, as I now see it, to reassure me—he claimed to remember it all. The only thing was—I'd invented the whole story there and then.

"There must have been something in my expression that gave me away, for he ended the conversation soon after and began to keep his distance from then on. He made sure there were other people around, so that we had no need to be alone—which suited my purpose, too, for I was now beginning to be deathly afraid of . . . I knew not what."

"Who were these 'other people' you spoke of?" Holmes asked quietly.

"Oh, there were a whole series of them who came and went and spent their time closeted with my guardian in his study. A few seemed to be regulars, almost like members of his staff—particularly that Professor James, a loathsome, oleaginous man, always toadying to him."

Holmes and I exchanged a covert glance at the name.

"Several of them were European. Sometimes when the study door opened and closed, I would hear snatches of French or German. I think to begin with he forgot that my French was fluent but he must have recalled the fact, because recently the conversation stops completely when someone enters or leaves."

"What did you hear them say?"

"There was talk of *une affaire incroyable* . . . it was *trop dangereuse*. Someone was arguing about *une détente globale, une guerre totale*. Some seemed to be excited by whatever they were planning but others were extremely frightened by it." She relaxed a little and her hands returned to their normal position in her lap. "I didn't know what to do, Mr. Holmes. I had no one to turn to. Sometimes I thought I was imagining it all but my 'feminine intuition', as you call it, told me I was not. That was how things stood when the three of us first met up at Loch Ness."

As she spoke, I recalled the moment with total clarity. If one can have a vision of a "vision", then that is what I experienced. Then Alicia's tone changed and she looked from one of us to the other in obvious distress. "It was then I realised that in some way you, Mr. Holmes, were involved in all this. Oh, not as part of whatever devilish scheme this man 'Moxton' . . ." She almost spat the word—"is hatching but in some complex, interwoven way I don't begin to understand. This man is obsessed with you. You are the only subject on which I have seen him less than icily calm. On the way back from Inverness he could talk of nothing else. Even the abominable Steel, who hangs on his every word, was losing his patience by the time we reached London."

"Tell us about Steel," Holmes prompted. "From

your tone I take it that there is little love lost between you?"

"That, I'm afraid, is the whole point," Alicia replied. "My arrival was clearly something he had not anticipated but as the weeks went by, he began to see how he could use my presence to advantage. I am not a vain woman, gentlemen, as my sex are apt to be. On the other hand, I know I am not unattractive."

She did not pause for comment and inwardly I blessed her for it.

"To cut a long story short, I detect that my 'guardian'—for I know not what else to call him—has decided that I would be a fit consort for Mr. Steel and has taken every occasion to throw us together on social occasions. You asked me to tell you about Steel . . ." She paused, as if what she was about to say would take an extra effort.

"Steel is Moxton's creature, Mr. Holmes, nothing more or less. Perhaps his Trojan Horse would be a more fitting description. What Moxton wants said but not attributed Steel says for him. He is present for most of these clandestine meetings and when he leaves at the end of the day, he struts out of there like a bantam cock. If Moxton could appoint him Prime Minister tomorrow, I believe that's precisely what he would do."

"And I believe that's precisely what he intends to try to do . . ." Holmes interjected. He then proceeded to fill in for Alicia most of the gaps between her story and what we had ourselves deduced of Moriarty's schemes. Frankly, I was surprised that he confided so much in someone he had met so recently but I have never known my friend to err in judgement on such matters. As he spoke I watched Alicia Creighton's face open like a morning flower and the sight was every bit as beautiful, as her premonitions began to make sense at last.

"But Mr. Holmes," she whispered, when he had delineated recent events with his usual precision, "this monster must be stopped at all costs. What can I do to help?"

"You have helped by coming here in the first place," my friend replied, "and you can help still further by returning there for a little while longer, while we gather the evidence we need to bring this man to book. And that, as you may surmise, will be no easy task. Moriarty is far too clever to soil his own hands and there is the further complication that he is now ostensibly an American citizen. One wrong move and the authorities will find themselves cocooned in diplomatic red tape. No, Alicia, at this moment you are our best and perhaps our last hope."

"But Holmes," I expostulated, "knowing what we now do, you can't ask this young lady to put herself into further danger. Now that Moriarty suspects."

"He may *suspect,* old fellow, but I fancy he is

more preoccupied with his master plan and, besides, in some small but significant way, Alicia is now part of it. Can't you see the *Clarion* trumpeting the doings of this glamorous first couple, once he has succeeded in placing Steel in the position of ultimate power? No, for the next few days at least we need her in the heart of the enemy camp—as your old Army friends would call it—gathering whatever intelligence she can of what Moriarty intends."

"You mean—a spy?"

For the first time I saw the playful schoolgirl inside the grown woman.

"Something of the sort," Holmes replied with a smile, "but I beg you most earnestly to take the utmost precautions. This man is more dangerous than you can possibly imagine. Your life will mean nothing to him, if he feels it poses the slightest threat to his plans. Watson or I will manage to keep in contact with you and, if you are in any doubt, call the nearest police constable for assistance. I will have Inspector Lestrade alert his men. One other thing, Alicia . . ."

"Yes, Mr. Holmes?"

"I think it is highly likely that you were followed here today. Whatever you do, when you leave, do not appear furtive or nervous in any way and, if your so-called guardian should challenge you, you simply came here to confirm our invitation to this evening's party." With that he rose and shook her firmly by the hand. "You are a brave woman and together the three of us will prevail."

I followed Holmes's example and tried to communicate through the subtle pressure of my hand on her how much I admired her spirit. Was it my imagination or was the pressure returned?

A few moments later the sound of the outer door closing signalled her departure. We resumed our chairs and sat in silence for a moment before I found my voice. "A woman of spirit, eh, Holmes?"

"Indeed," he replied. "I can only think of one other who compares."

A pause and then he caught my eye. "Under normal circumstances, old fellow, I would feel it my bounden duty to lecture you on the need to regard the client as strictly an objective element in the greater puzzle. I should probably elaborate on the danger an emotional involvement posed to proper reasoning, go on to warn you of the particular dangers posed by the female of the species and end by telling you how the most charming woman I ever encountered was taken to the scaffold for poisoning three small children for their insurance money . . . However, under the circumstances I see all too clearly before me, I shall refrain . . ."

Then, after another moment's thought, he picked up his pistol and weighed it thoughtfully in his hand. "So now we have another reason to bring this business to a speedy conclusion."

CHAPTER EIGHT

The house in Chester Square was illuminated like a stage set as the hansom dropped me at the front door that evening. And indeed, the press of people in their various costumes streaming in through the elegant front doors had all the appearance of a pantomime curtain call.

I saw numerous "Alices", complete with long blonde hair and I reflected that the town's wig-makers must have been doing a roaring trade all day to cope with the demand. I was not as familiar with Carroll's book as Holmes clearly was but I could recognise several March Hares, White Rabbits and Duchesses with pig babies, a good sprinkling of Mad Hatters, Kings and Queens of Hearts as well as various other ambulant playing cards. I myself, having never had much of a taste for making more of a fool of myself in public than I can help, had settled for what I hoped was a fairly discreet Red King. With Mrs. Hudson's aid I had swathed myself in some red material she had found in one of her many bottom drawers, kept for who knows what eventual purpose. A cardboard crown from a local fancy dress emporium and an old assegai some Army friend had left me completed my wardrobe. To say that I felt foolish would be putting it mildly. Just as

Mrs. Hudson had put the finishing touches to this rather *outré* ensemble, Holmes had emerged from his bedroom still wearing his old dressing gown. Seeing the expression on my face, he raised a placatory hand.

"I know what you're thinking, old fellow, but I shall be there, you have my word on it. However, something has just come up which requires my attention and, since it is imperative that we observe this evening's events most carefully, I would consider it a great personal favour if you would precede me . . ."

Having been left to storm more than one citadel single-handed in the past, I was naturally sceptical, but the expression on his face was enough to convince me of his sincerity so, with a certain amount of huffing and puffing—and Mrs. Hudson's assurance that she'd never seen anything quite like it, really she hadn't—I allowed myself to be escorted down to the cab.

Now here I was—feeling, I must admit, a little more comfortable in the company of dozens of others who were clearly feeling equally ridiculous—walking up the steps to the front door, where liveried servants wearing frog masks—(the Frog Footmen, what else?) were waiting to receive them.

No sooner had I passed into the main hallway than I felt a hand on my arm and a voice hissed: "Over here, Doctor" in my ear. As I was pulled behind a convenient pillar I saw that I was being addressed by an insignificant little man wearing a large walrus moustache.

"By George Lestrade!" I exclaimed, "that's an incredible disguise!"

"But I'm not *wearing* a disguise," he said, looking puzzled for a moment. Then, fingering his upper lip, "*Oh, you mean this? Yes, it is rather subtle, isn't it? Less is more, Doctor, less is more. The Walrus, see? All I need now is a Carpenter . . . and a few oysters, of course!"* And he laughed so much that he almost choked on his facial hair.

Then, sensing that I was in no mood for such half-baked pleasantries, he added seriously: "Mr. 'Olmes coming along later, is he? You don't surprise me. He'll want us to act as an advance guard to distract 'em like. Very much like he did in that case of . . ."

"I don't think Mr. Holmes's actions need concern you, Lestrade. As you should know well by now, Mr. Holmes has his own way of doing things."

I was about to enlarge on my friend's eminently successful *modus operandi* and compare it with Lestrade's own pedestrian methods when there was a single stroke on a gong and the room fell silent.

"Good evening, ladies and gentlemen, and welcome to Wonderland!"

At the top of the sweeping staircase stood one of the most remarkable figures I can remember seeing and not for the first time in recent days did I have the feeling that we were all characters in some strange fantasy of someone else's creation. Moxton—as I had to think of him for this evening at least—had dressed himself as Humpty Dumpty. Through the costume maker's art he contrived to look like a perfect oval with a smiling face peeping out. Despite the bulk of it, his costume was made of some pliant material that allowed him to move about freely. There was no doubt that if he intended to dominate the proceedings, he had certainly succeeded. I remembered the exchange between him and Holmes by the loch side and Moxton quoting the line—"The question is . . . which is to be master, that's all." There was no longer any question.

"And now, ladies and gentlemen, the Frog Footmen will lead you in to dinner."

With that he began to navigate the staircase with some care and, as he moved from the landing, I could see standing right behind him a young couple.

Had their expressions matched their appearance, they would have been nothing less than spectacular but Royston Steel's lips were set in the rictus of a smile for public consumption and Alicia's face could have been carved out of alabaster. As they descended in Moxton's wake he tucked her arm under his in a manner that brooked no resistance.

He was dressed as the Knave of Hearts in a sort of doublet and hose with a playing card woven into the front of it and a flat vaguely medieval hat. I was sure, on reflection, that my description was doing him an injustice. Mr. Steel's costume would have been designed with Sir John Tenniel's *Alice* illustrations firmly in mind.

Alicia might have stepped out of the very same engraving. The only difference was that her hair, instead of being blonde, was raven black and brushed straight back from her forehead to fall to her waist. The child's dress with its puffed sleeves and layered skirt made her look like a mirror image of the girl who had inspired this whole dream world we were all now inhabiting.

"Quite a looker, eh, Doctor?" It was the peasant Lestrade at my elbow. I was about to address him in no uncertain terms when I remembered the delicacy of Alicia's situation in this house. The last thing any of us needed was to call undue attention to ourselves. I bit back my reply. Just at that moment a Frog Footman who was obviously high in the pecking order—if frogs can peck—appeared at our shoulders. "Gentlemen, if I might conduct you to your places. Doctor Watson and Inspector Lestrade, if I am not mistaken? This way, gentlemen." And then to Lestrade—"An elegantly understated costume, if I may say so,

Inspector. So few people know when to leave well alone." I had no need to look at Lestrade to know that he was puffing himself up with pride.

"Y'see, Doctor, what did I tell you?"

I did, however, glance at the Frog Footman and noticed that he had a particularly patrician appearance. Possibly a butler earning extra money on an evening off. Portly in bearing with a nose that would have done duty on a Roman coin. Precisely the sort of chap that always makes me feel I've forgotten to do something vital. I tried to convey a degree of *hauteur* by the set of my shoulders as we entered the dining room, where by now most of the other guests were already seated. Lestrade and I found ourselves seated on either side of a formidable Queen of Hearts, who was clearly enjoying every minute of her new incarnation. Her small talk was negligible—not that mine is anything to write home about—but whenever the conversation flagged, she would cry—"Off with his head!" and collapse into hysterical laughter. I found it increasingly difficult to join in until I heard her ask Lestrade—"And what are you supposed to be?"

Whatever he might have been inclined to answer, he was saved the necessity by Moxton rising to his feet, insofar as his costume allowed one to gauge whether he was sitting or standing, and tapping his wine glass with a fork. It was clear the man was about to make yet another speech. Holmes had always told me that Moriarty had been singularly monosyllabic but the reincarnated Moxton was more than making up for that deficiency.

"Ladies and gentlemen," said Humpty Dumpty, "may I introduce you to a few of our distinguished guests this evening?" He then proceeded to pick out a number of people dotted around the various tables and say a few words about each, before asking the subject of each eulogy to rise and acknowledge the polite applause. A Mad Hatter turned out to be a far eastern potentate, Bill the Lizard a distinguished couturier, a hirsute Duchess the doyenne of a country seat, and so on. I had settled into a comfortable routine of applauding while letting my mind roam else-where, principally in the direction of the top table where Alice/Alicia was toying with her food when I heard my own name.

". . . and I cannot forebear to mention the friend and associate of the famous consulting detective, Mr. Sherlock Holmes (who, alas, appears to be unable to join us this evening) . . ." I made a mental note to settle that score with Holmes the minute I got back to Baker Street. "The man who has enshrined the legend in his own vivid prose—his Boswell, Dr. John H. Watson!" At that I heard a round of applause which, I must admit, was rather gratifying and only slightly spoiled by Lestrade's loud *sotto voce*—"They also serve who only stand and wait, eh, Doctor?"

"Now," Humpty Dumpty continued, "in the true tradition of Wonderland we have, so to speak, had our cake marked 'Eat Me' . . ." There was an outburst of loud and slightly forced laughter from those who recognised the reference, which was quickly joined by those who realised that they should. "I should now like to propose a toast to all of you. In front of you you will find a small bottle marked . . ."

As with one voice the guests shouted out . . .

"Drink Me!"

"Exactly. What a well read group you are!" Gales of sycophantic laughter. "Now I am going to ask our Guest of Honour, our *primus inter pares*, if you will—the Home Secretary here . . ."

At that point the whole scene seemed to freeze for me and I had an overwhelming sense of dread. Something was about to go horribly wrong here in this gilded hall with its glittering chandeliers and its mirrored walls multiplying our images until the room and its occupants seem to stretch to infinity.

For a moment Moxton seemed to be mouthing in silence, as I stared at the man sitting next to him, smiling up at him with an expression of foolish pleasure.

Sir Giles Broadbent, QC was not renowned for his piercing intelligence and there were those who said he was not long for his present office.

Sitting there, dressed as the Dormouse, complete with a patch of fur and whiskers adorning his somewhat protuberant nose, he looked positively ridiculous but something forbade me to look at him in that light.

Now Moxton was coming to the point—"ask my Right Honourable Friend to propose the toast to The Guests."

Rising rather unsteadily to his feet the Dormouse reached for the tiny bottle I had noticed earlier set by every place. An exact copy from the book, it resembled a small medicine bottle with a paper label tied around the neck on which was printed in large letters—DRINK ME. Even now I could see the other guests picking up theirs and removing the stopper for the Toast.

The Home Secretary held his aloft and peered myopically around the room. Then without preamble he said, somewhat slurrily—"I give you—The Geshtst!"—and drained the bottle. With that he sat down heavily, made a small whimpering sound, and fell forward with his head in his dessert plate.

For a moment the huge room fell silent Then Humpty Dumpty stepped into the breach. Rising to his feet and indicating his dormant guest of honour, he said—"The Dormouse is asleep again." At which there was some laughter in which I could detect a mixture of nervousness and relief.

The laughter soon began to subside, however, when Moxton said nothing more but continued to look with what appeared to be increasing anxiety at the figure slumped next to him. Now people were turning to each other and a subdued buzz began to grow. Lestrade leaned across the Queen of Hearts and muttered—"Doctor, is this in the book, do you know?" I shook my head dumbly.

It was then that I became aware of sudden activity at the top table. The patrician Frog Footman who had shown Lestrade and me to our places must have been standing just behind the guests, for he was now purposefully man-handling the Dormouse back into a sitting position. The sight of a grown man wearing a mouse's nose and with his face covered in raspberry trifle should have been ludicrous but somehow no one was laughing.

Then the Frog Butler spoke. "Is there a doctor in the house?"

Instinct propelled me to my feet and across the few feet to the top table. I had the impression of open mouths and fixed stares all around me and then I was bending over the Home Secretary. On one side of me bobbed Humpty Dumpty, as if he were on a spring. On the other I was aware of the impassive butler. All of which faded into the background when a distinctive odour reached me.

"Exactly, Watson. Burnt almonds. Cyanide."

It was Holmes's voice but before I could react it

continued in a low tone only audible to me. "Don't whatever you do, look in my direction. Meet me in the Crystal Room later." Then, in a voice intended to be heard by Moxton at least— "Do you wish me to alert the constabulary, sir? I believe an Inspector Lestrade is among those present?"

"At once, my good man," I replied authoritatively, beginning to enjoy the situation as much as the presence of death would permit. Then, turning to Moxton, I said so that the whole room could hear—"I advise you to contact Whitehall and Scotland Yard right away. The Home Secretary has been murdered!"

Pandemonium. Then, determined to keep control of the proceedings for as long as possible, I called out—"Inspector Lestrade, over here, if you please."

Lestrade made his way over to us with a gravitas made less than impressive only by his outsized moustache. I turned to the butler, only to find that he had melted away as completely as the Cheshire Cat, leaving not even a smile behind. Within moments, it seemed, the room was full of uni-formed policemen and I learned later that Lestrade had stationed them in the nearby Regent's Park to be ready for any eventuality.

Seeing that everyone seemed to be fully occupied, I began to make an unobtrusive exit in search of the Crystal Room. The only person who noticed my stratagem was Alicia whose expression seemed to convey a combination of concern and compassion. I could have sworn her lips mimed "Good luck" as I sidled from the room.

It took me little time to find the Crystal Room, which also opened off the main hall. Whoever had built this mansion had clearly been of a narcissistic persuasion. Like the dining room, the place was mirrored but this time the glass went from floor to ceiling. The effect was like being in one of those fairground Halls of Mirrors.

I confess I found it more than a little unnerving to confront endless effigies of a not particularly impressive middle-aged medico attired from head to foot in a ridiculous red get-up and a cardboard crown that, in the excitement of recent events, I had forgotten to discard.

"Most impressive, Watson," I heard a familiar voice say. From the depths of a large club armchair with its back to the door emerged the figure of Holmes, his butler's attire discarded in favour of his normal dark suit. "All that is needed is for me to acquire a matching outfit in white and we can re-enact the Musgrave Ritual on high days and holidays."

Then, taking my arm and pulling me further into the room away from the possibility of prying ears—"You must concede, old fellow, that I kept my word. Forgive the duplicity but I felt that I would learn more from being on the inside looking out than on the outside looking in."

"And did you?"

"Indeed, I did. I learned that you can hide an extra servant at a party as effectively as you can hide a leaf in a forest. And if that servant assumes a certain seniority, there is even less likelihood of his presence being questioned. You know, I think I might quite enjoy being a butler—without, of course, the encumbrance of the aquatic livery. It is very refreshing to see so much ready acquiescence.

"But come, Watson, there is much to be done. So far we have all been playing our assigned parts in Moriarty's charade but this evening that game is over. He has crossed his personal Rubicon through murder . . ."

"I wonder if one *can* cross the Rubicon on the way to Waterloo? It sounds like an interesting diversion, to say the least."

I suddenly realised that we were not alone. Dominating the room were dozens of images of Humpty Dumpty and his grotesque smile. "Good evening, Holmes. May I congratulate you on your 'performance'. I thought you were a little slow with the Montrachet but otherwise . . . Let me know if you ever need a reference. In a little while you very well may."

"Good evening, Moriarty. I'm sure you won't mind if—within the privacy of these however many walls I don't indulge your little game any further?"

"Be my guest—and you, too, Doctor—for the time being at least. Later? Who can say? But you must admit it is rather an amusing game, isn't it? You're a musician, Holmes. Think of it as a symphony. So far we've enjoyed a few little trills to settle the audience in their seats. Tonight it was time to introduce one of the main themes. Discordant to some ears, perhaps, but then taste is such a personal matter, don't you find?"

"And what do you call your damned symphony?" I found myself shouting.

"Oh, I would have thought it was fairly obvious, old fellow," said Holmes, as cool as the proverbial cucumber. "Moriarty's Unfinished Symphony."

"But very soon to be finished, gentlemen—and way beyond your pathetic power to stop, Holmes. This will not be some unseemly scuffle in the middle of nowhere. You are dealing now with forces as elemental as the human psyche. Your common man in the street—the supposed object of everyone's good intentions—is fundamentally a fool. He wants what I provide for him and he will want what I am about to provide—once he gets used to it. The process is so inevitable and irreversible that I don't mind your knowing about it. In fact, I always intended that you should . . ."

"But there has been murder here tonight," I said and even as I spoke the words they sounded strangely irrelevant even to my own ears.

"Murder, ah yes, so there has. Was it not you

116

yourself, Holmes, who spoke so eloquently of the 'scarlet thread of murder running through the colourless skein of life'? But murder? I would prefer the term 'execution'—the execution of an incompetent. The first, I fear, of many such.

"But I'm afraid that when they come to investigate this 'murder', all Inspector Lestrade's men will find are a series of *culs-de-sac*. So many strangers have had the run of the house and after all, who can tell where the hired help comes from these days?" And he gave Holmes a lopsided smile. "How can one be sure they are even who they say they are? No, my own opinion—which I shall be sharing with the world in tomorrow's *Clarion*—is that this whole unfortunate affair may be laid at the door of the international terrorist conspiracy that is polluting so much of the free world and which this government is clearly powerless to stop. And I think you will find that people will see things my way.

"Was it not my fellow American, Mark Twain, who observed that despite the best efforts of Britain's preachers and statesmen to draw the two countries together in friendship and mutual respect, the newspapers 'with what seems a steady and calculated purpose', I seem to remember him saying—'discourage this'—I love the 'steady and calculated purpose'! 'The newspapers,' he concluded, 'are going to win this fight.' And who am I to argue with Mark Twain?

"You see, my dear Holmes, this time nobody will listen to any accusations you may try to bring. They will prefer my plot. The world has changed around you but you have not changed with it, because you do not choose to comprehend the forces that have been unleashed. I no longer need to eliminate you. The winds of change will blow you out of my path like a dead leaf. In some strange way I have to confess that I have always felt our destinies to be somehow linked. It is simply my sense of dramatic symmetry that requires me to have you there to witness my triumph.

"But I must not delay you further. Thank you for attending my opening night."

Then, as suddenly as he had appeared, Humpty Dumpty was gone. One moment there were multiple images of this grotesque egg-shaped figure, for all the world like the fragments in a kaleidoscope. The next, we were alone. I imagine he must have used some hidden door in one of the mirrors but all I know is that his disappearance—like his arrival—was an illusion that would not have disgraced the great Maskelyne. I looked at Holmes. Instead of concern I saw what I can only describe as excitement. The man was enjoying this bizarre and deadly game. His eyes were positively afire as he hurried me from this Hall of Mirrors.

"Come, Watson. Time for Act Two, I think . . ."

CHAPTER NINE

W hat do you mean—Act Two?" It was the following morning and I was becoming more than a little frustrated with Holmes's lack of communication. Often in the past he had gone off into a brown study when a case was reaching its crisis. Nonetheless, I still found his attitude lacking in consideration. Did he not think after all these years that I could keep my own council?

Events had proceeded very much as predicted after our return from the Chester Square party. As we left the atmosphere was very different from the one I had found. Guests were leaving in dribs and drabs after what I suspected was some fairly perfunctory questioning by Lestrade and his men. We knew, after all, who was responsible for the Home Secretary's murder but it was still necessary to be seen to be going through the usual routine procedures. Finery that had looked so cheerful and gay a few short hours ago now clung to the departing revellers like so many bedraggled feathers.

The moment we regained the warmth and safety of Baker Street, I threw my own costume in a corner, fastened my favourite smoking jacket firmly around me and settled into my chair for a comforting pipe of Arcadia, while I tried to make sense of all I had seen and heard.

Holmes—as I had known him do on so many occasions in the past—sat curled up in his own chair, his head wreathed in the smoke from his favourite black clay pipe. Every now and then those aquiline features would emerge like a graven image, only to fade again. I was reminded of one of those psychic manifestations the papers had been debating lately. Then I realised that this particular manifestation was speaking.

"Do you not find it curious, Watson, that criminals of talent—even of the genius, which I feel we must allow to Moriarty—can never seem to avoid the compulsion to annotate their plans?

"As part of my duties as the Professor's admittedly temporary butler, I felt it incumbent upon me to tidy the desk in his study. Oh, and by the way, I see he still cannot bear to part from his Greuze—you remember that oil of the girl with her head on her hands? A pretty piece, totally wasted on him. Anyway, there in the locked bottom right hand drawer—a hiding place I seem to remember he favoured in his previous incarnation—I found his *Journal*. So many people seem doomed to be creatures of habits— for which, I suppose, the consulting detective must be duly grateful."

I looked around the room as he spoke. There was the old Persian slipper crammed with his favourite tobacco, the cigar in the coal scuttle, the jack knife transfixing unanswered correspondence to the mantelpiece with the engraving of the Reichenbach Falls above it, the commonplace books that appeared random but on which he could lay an unerring hand in a moment . . . all of the artifacts of a life that had remained untouched (and if he had had his way, undusted) even throughout his enforced absence. If *anyone* was a creature of habit it was Sherlock Holmes!

Holmes interrupted my reverie by taking a scrap of folded paper out of the pocket of his dressing gown. "I'll even wager he's using the same mathematical code. Once a mathematician, always a mathematician . . ."

He picked up a pad and pencil from a nearby table and began to jot down a series of notes while consulting the paper. I thought I heard him mutter under his breath something about it being an insult to a man who had written a monograph identifying a hundred and sixty separate ciphers to be given this child's play. Finally, he sat back in his chair, tapping his right forefinger against his mouth thoughtfully.

"Mycroft is right, old fellow, we are sailing into stormy waters indeed. Even a cursory examination of these annotations is enough to indicate that Moriarty is in close contact with some highly dangerous people, none of whom wish our country well. In the last two weeks alone he appears to have had several meetings with both 'IZ' and 'HvB'. Now, unless I miss my guess, Watson, 'IZ' stands for Ilya Zokov, the notorious Russian Nihilist on whose head the Czar has put a price that would keep you in comfort to a ripe old age and allow me to retire and keep bees. And 'HvB' is even more interesting. Heinrich von Bork, a rising man in German Military intelligence, currently Imperial Envoy and close to Kaiser Wilhelm. Uncomfortable bedfellows at first glance. I very much fear that in their different ways both Mycroft and Moriarty are right in predicting that Europe and very possibly the rest of the world is drifting towards some sort of cataclysm. Perhaps the most we can hope to do is to delay that progress until this country has time to prepare. And to do even that we shall have to strain every sinew.

"Hello, that will be Lestrade . . ."

Down below the front door bell rang and we heard a few murmured words from Mrs. Hudson before the familiar clump of the Inspector's boots on the stairs.

It was a dejected Lestrade who was shown in. Even the loss of the lugubrious moustache did little to cheer his expression. "You were quite right, Mr. 'Olmes. We found the bottle of cyanide in the pocket of one of the waiters in the cloak-room. Young French chap, obviously scared out of his wits. The bottle had been wiped clean, of course. I took him in for questioning but more as a formality than anything else. It's pretty clear that it was planted where we were sure to find it. I can't get over the gall of that Moxton feller. He must think we're stupid or something."

"To be fair, Lestrade, we haven't given him any reason so far to think otherwise. That situation, however, is about to change."

Lestrade opened his mouth to say something but I could have told him to save his breath. With his consummate sense of theatre our principal actor was not about to give any more encores this evening. After a few more civilities on my part, I saw the Inspector to the door and retired for the night, leaving Holmes to smoke as many pipes as he thought fit in splendid isolation. My last glimpse of him was of him leaning back with his head sunk in the cushion of his chair, the half-closed eyes belying the activity within that teeming brain. The following morning, as I have indicated, I pursued my attack. "Come along now, Holmes—what do you mean . . . a Second Act? And what part have I been assigned, pray?"

"Well, my dear chap, I would suggest a leisurely lunch at your club, a post-prandial stroll through St. James's Park—the weather looks as though it should hold—and then I've managed to get you a ticket for the opening night of *La Bohème* at Covent Garden. You'll find it waiting for you at the box office. I'm afraid no one of consequence is singing but Puccini is always good for a tune or two, though personally I prefer a bit of Teutonic Sturm und Drang, as you know."

"Are you serious, Holmes?" I began to splutter, when he added—"Oh, and when the performance is over, you might do me the favour of strolling over to that other Palace of Varieties, the House of Commons. There is to be a speech by the Right Honourable Mr. Royston Steel on which I would particularly value your opinion. On this occasion Mycroft has made the necessary arrangements."

Once the idea had sunk in, I must admit it did have a certain charm. If Holmes thought there was nothing more to do for the time being, who was I to argue?

After the stress of the past few days, lunch at the club was decidedly pleasant. I ran into several old chums and we exchanged our theories of how to prevent the country from going to the dogs over a very fair lamb chop and a more than decent bottle of Beaune. After which I took the prescribed stroll through the park, where a spell of unseasonably late sunshine was tempting London's usual cross section of humanity to temporarily forget their differences and share God's good fresh air. Perhaps the Beaune had a certain something to do with my sense of wellbeing but I found myself thinking that each of these very different people had their own joys and sadnesses, which they had to arrange every day into the best possible pattern. The pattern they made might not be perfect but it was their pattern to make—not one imposed upon them by some outside force.

I decided there and then that whatever I, a simple retired army doctor, could do to defend that right I would do, whatever the cost. Not all the important battles were fought on a field of battle. I also reflected how clever it was of my friend, Sherlock Holmes to create the time for me to come to that conclusion.

As he himself would attest, when I get an idea into my head, I tend to be as tenacious with it as the bull pup I once owned. For the rest of the day I found myself thinking about the magnitude of the fraud Moriarty was perpetrating and with what apparent ease someone with nerve and resource could distract public attention from what he was truly about. I also found myself worrying about the part we were asking a certain young lady to play in this deadly business.

With thoughts like these racing through my brain, I barely took in the fact that the opera I found myself watching later that evening was *La Bohème*. Then Puccini's soaring romanticism suddenly took on a whole new meaning and when the tenor began *Che gelida manina*, I vowed that, if this ugly business were ever brought to a conclusion, by way of celebration, I would invite a certain young lady to occupy the seat next to me and share these glorious sounds with me.

It must have been close to eleven o'clock when I found myself approaching the House of Commons. Although I had passed by those familiar buildings more times than I could possibly recall, I have to confess I had never been inside them and, therefore, had no knowledge of their layout. Consequently, it took me some little time and helpful direction from several policemen on duty before I arrived at the entrance to the Visitors' Gallery.

As Holmes had anticipated, Mycroft had duly worked his magic and the attendants handed over a pass with my name on it in elegant copperplate script. By the time I had laboured up the stairs and passed through the doors into the Gallery itself, I was more than a little flustered. The thought had just sunk in that I had not the faintest idea what I was doing here. As I had done so often in the past, I had accepted Holmes's instructions unquestioningly.

It was only then that I realised I was alone in the Gallery and I wryly reflected on the very real influence Mycroft must have exerted to achieve such a result. The noise from the debating chamber below brought my thoughts into focus.

In the press of the day's events it had not even occurred to me to discover what the topic of the debate might be about. Now it rapidly became clear that there was at least as much drama being enacted on this stage as I had witnessed earlier in the evening, although with rather less tuneful result.

From what I could immediately glean, the topic under discussion was national security and feelings were clearly running high. Several times as I was trying to identify the various speakers I heard impassioned mention of the *Clarion*'s coverage of recent events. In answer to one specific question the man I identified as the newly-appointed Home Secretary murmured something almost inaudible about the need to protect the essential freedom of the Press—only to be jeered at from the Opposition back benches.

"Helped you get your job, didn't it?"

It took the Speaker several minutes of serious gavel pounding to restore some semblance of order to the emotional maelstrom the hallowed Chamber had become.

As the debate—if such it could be dignified—continued, it became increasingly clear to me that underlying the anger was a genuine fear. These men, some of them vastly experienced statesmen of world renown, were manifestly out of their depth. They were faced with a situation totally outside their experience—and they did not know what to do! If I needed further proof that Moriarty's scheme was working, I was witnessing a perfect example of it in action.

My philosophical reverie was dramatically broken by what happened next. By now it had become virtually impossible for any speaker to say more than a few words before being interrupted by abusive call and counter-call from across the floor of the House.

But now a new figure was rising to his feet and the noise began to subside. It was clear that members of both parties wanted to hear what Royston Steel had to say.

The man cut an impressive figure, I have to admit. Tall and sleek and with an arrogant curl to his mouth, he paused like an actor waiting for his audience to settle down. I find it hard to believe that any of the orators in that gathering— many of whose names were household words— could have exerted the same power over the mob that our elected representatives had become as Steel did that day.

Then he began to speak . . .

. . . and as he did, you could feel the collective blood run cold. For the words the man spoke were the ravings of a madman, made all the more frightening by the cold, intelligent, apparently reasoned way he spoke them. He began by castigating the various races, colours and creeds he said were insidiously undermining our country.

"Maggots in the fabric," I remember him saying. There was a certain amount of tentative nodding and a muffled "Hear! Hear!" from the shires, but soon even that stopped. There was something viciously racist in phrases like "the serpentine Levantine" that reduced that opinionated group to an uncomfortable silence.

Then Steel turned to "the enemy within," all those who were plotting to sell their own country to "the semite and the barbarian" and others who were "ethnically inferior."

Now he began to lace his accusations with the names of individuals, many of whom were in this very Chamber. These men were traitors who should not be allowed the luxury of resignation but should be tried and, when found guilty, executed for treason.

By now the shock was wearing off. I had the distinct feeling that for the first part of his speech many of his audience had thought the man must be staging some sort of elaborate and extended joke and that at some point he would let them all in on it. Perhaps he was parodying some admittedly extreme points of view in order to discredit them. But this was now all too obviously not the case. Angry murmurs began to reverberate around the hall.

Steel himself seemed to be losing his icy composure. The voice was louder and the gestures wilder. Parliament should be disbanded, the Monarchy banished. A few men of vision that he had already hand-picked could lead Britain out of the mire of shabby corruption. Yes, there would be sacrifices, cankers would have to be ruthlessly cut out but then a racially pure society, a greater Great Britain would be ready to cross the sea and emulate Henry at Agincourt. Today Britain, tomorrow Europe . . . then why not the world? As he reached his peroration, he began to throw up one hand in a demented militaristic sort of salute. He was screaming in an effort to be heard above the tumult in the Chamber.

Members on both sides of the House were on their feet, howling and shaking their fists and order papers at Steel in one of the rare moments of unanimity Parliament has ever seen. Several of the more agile Members began to clamber over the Tory benches in an obvious attempt to reach Steel and do him physical harm and it was at that point that I noticed some counter movement at one end of the room. For some time the Speaker had been trying to make himself heard in an effort to ask Steel to withdraw. Realising the effort was futile, he had clearly signalled for the attendants to perform a duty that had hardly ever proved necessary in the history of that august assembly. Now the black garbed attendants were forcing their way through the gesticulating Members of Parliament for the purpose of removing one of them from the seat of government.

It was the saving of Steel, there is no doubt in my mind about that. His harangue had turned a group of civilised and reasonably orderly men into a mob that would not have disgraced the French Revolution. All that was missing were the tumbrils and the guillotine and bare hands looked ready to make good the difference.

As if the whole thing were happening in slow motion, the attendants parted the crowd like the Red Sea, surrounded Steel—who now seemed calm and quite content to be taken into custody—and suddenly they were gone, as if they had never been. The floor of the Chamber below me was left a seething cauldron of emotion and noise, with old enemies for once united in a common—or perhaps I should say, decidedly uncommon—cause.

It was a sight I never expect to see again and an extremely disturbing one, the more I thought about it. What one person and the weapon of words could achieve!

It was clear that there was nothing more to be seen here. I hurried down the stairs to try and see the end of this remarkable affair, in time to see the distinctive police carriage move away from the gate and the black clad attendants begin to file back into the building. Holmes's criticisms of police efficiency were a little harsh on occasions like this, I thought. Nothing could have been smoother or more expeditious than the way Steel's exit had been handled. Even the gatekeeper wished me good evening as calmly as if we had both just been witness to an everyday occurrence.

I decided to walk for a while as I tried to sort my thoughts into some kind of order. I had just watched a man commit political suicide. Whether the words he had uttered were those of someone in the grip of some sudden seizure or whether there was some other explanation was irrelevant. Nothing could expunge those vile sentiments from the minds and hearts of those who had heard them—and on the morrow the rest of the world would share that disgust. How could a man whose reputation had been built to so great a degree on the golden opinions of the Press fall into such an obvious trap? And what would this do to Moriarty's schemes? Was it in some bizarre way part of those schemes? None of it made sense, I concluded and hailed a passing cab.

As I opened the front door of 221B I could hear the murmur of conversation from the room above. I hastened up the familiar stairs. Holmes would be anxious to know how I had fared on my mission.

"Holmes, the most amazing thing . . ." I said, as I entered the room . . . to find Mycroft Holmes ensconced in my chair and Holmes's place occupied by—Royston Steel.

CHAPTER TEN

Y ou may cease and desist from your celebrated impersonation of a fish, old fellow. And please shut the door. There is an infernal draught in here. I must have a word with Mrs. Hudson."

It was Steel who spoke—with the voice of Sherlock Holmes!

As if in response, Mycroft rumbled from the depths of his—my chair.

" 'The time has come,' the Walrus said, 'to talk of many things . . .' "

"But—but—I saw you, I mean, Steel, in the House only a few minutes ago . . ."

"No, Watson, you saw but you did not observe . . ." Holmes was now pulling off the sleek black wig and the face putty that had once again transformed his features and allowed him temporarily to inhabit someone else's skin. As he towelled his face vigorously with the cloth Mycroft tossed to him, he continued—"You were in Steel's milieu. You *expected* to see Steel. *Ergo*, you saw him. As did everyone else. In the past most of them had taken him for granted, an irrelevant irritant. Tonight they took notice— and they will never forget him."

Thinking back to the performance I had seen little more than an hour ago, I knew, of course, that he was right. Not for the first time I reflected that when Holmes put on a disguise he did not impersonate, he *became* his subject. He transformed his appearance, his bearing—even, I suspect, his soul.

I looked at him. He had the contented look I imagine comes over every actor at the conclusion of a performance that has clearly impressed his audience. Finally I managed to say—"But Holmes, you were masterly. You *were* the man . . ."

"Thank you, Watson. It's good to know the skills I picked up in America as a young man have not totally atrophied. Oh, have I never related that part of my pre-Watson existence? Remind me to do so when we have rather more leisure. It may serve to pad out one of your more lurid tales."

Suddenly a thought struck me.

"But what about the real Steel," I stammered, "suppose he had walked in while you were impersonating him?"

"I have too much confidence in my brother's ability to exert his personality when he so chooses," Holmes replied, looking in that direction. Mycroft acknowledged the compliment with the merest inclination of his head.

"Mycroft intimated that there were those in the highest echelons of the Government who would value Steel's opinion on matters of national importance. To ensure security the meeting was arranged away from prying eyes in the privacy of Mycroft's private rooms with catering provided by the Diogenes Club opposite. So tell us, Mycroft, what state secrets did you manage to impart?"

"I'm afraid that, owing to the excitement of entertaining so distinguished a guest, I was a little carried away. As I recall, the conversation barely moved beyond the topic of Coptic scrolls and how they might conceivably undermine the very foundations of revealed religion—a topic which seemed to exercise Mr. Steel considerably as the evening wore on."

"I told Mycroft to keep him occupied until I knew his name would have been called to speak. I was fairly sure that what he would have to say was likely to produce a certain—shall we say?— *frisson*."

"That it certainly did," I attested fervently. "I thought they were about to lynch him—you. It reminded me of some of the accounts I've read of the French Revolution. You could have cut the emotion in the House with a knife. But gentlemen, put my simple mind at rest—what precisely was the *point* of it?"

"A riposte in the battle for the hearts and minds of the British people," Mycroft replied gravely.

"I'm not sure I'd pitch it with quite such *gravitas*," Holmes added. "While the 'British people' are undoubtedly possessed of both, they scarcely consider them in those elevated terms—at least, not in my observation. No, Watson, in simpler terms my aim was to put a spoke in Moriarty's wheel and that we have undoubtedly done. He was expecting some sort of frontal counter-attack and had prepared his defences accordingly. Yet any student of his methods—and I flatter myself that I am one—knows that our dear Professor's *modus operandi* contains one unifying thread. He never soils his own hands with the minutiae of the execution of his plans. Therefore, he is vulnerable through his minions.

"Removing Steel—for be in no doubt we have done just that—may be no more than a temporary inconvenience, as I say, a mere spoke in the wheel of Moriarty's plan but in a complex piece of machinery one wheel meshes in with the working of another and another, so that a change of speed may lead to disaster for the whole machine. More important, we have shown Moriarty that his plans are capable of disruption. Perhaps just as galling for a man of his vanity will be this . . ."

And he picked up a piece of paper from the table next to him and handed it to me. "He thought that only he was ingenious enough to pursue his course with one hand and orchestrate his literary conceit with the other. He now knows differently . . ." On the paper was printed in Holmes's distinctive hand . . .

TWEEDLEDUM AND TWEEDLEDEE
AGREED TO HAVE A BATTLE
FOR TWEEDLEDUM SAID
  TWEEDLEDEE
HAD SPOILED HIS NICE NEW RATTLE

Below the quotation was the familiar face of the Cheshire Cat but this time its grin was upside down, giving it a faintly sinister, Oriental appearance.

"That will appear in all of tomorrow's newspapers—including the *Clarion*—as my private message to Moriarty. But the main message, which those same papers will carry free and *gratis* was the one I delivered earlier this evening and which you, Watson, were good enough by your unfeigned reaction to authenticate. The Right Honourable Members saw Tweedledee—but they *thought* they saw Tweedledum and it is on him that they will vent their anger and frustration. Tonight was just as much of an execution as the one Moriarty contrived yesterday—except that on this occasion the victim lived. Only one man will truly appreciate the—if I may employ the pun—*double entendre . . .*"

And allowing himself a small whisper of a smile, Holmes settled back in his chair and completed his toilet. "I think we might safely say that the price of steel has just gone down."

I could not forebear to state what seemed to

me to be obvious. "But tomorrow Steel will deny that he was present in the House and explain where he really was . . ."

"So he will," Holmes replied, "but who will believe him? *He* knows he dined with Mycroft and now you and I know but the rest of the world will assume he is merely trying to avoid the consequences of his actions. After all, several hundred of our leading citizens have the evidence of their own eyes and they are not likely to admit the possibility of error. We have simply turned Moriarty's weaponry upon himself. QED.

"Tonight we witnessed Act Two—or perhaps that dignifies it too much. Let us say an *entracte*. We must now possess our souls in patience until we see what Moriarty does next."

The impact of the evening's events suddenly seemed to hit me and I found myself stifling a yawn.

"Well, gentlemen, if you will excuse me," I said, "I think I'll possess my soul by having a good night's sleep."

As I left the room, I could again hear the murmur of their conversation, as each completed the other's sentences. With two such minds working in concert, what chance did an antagonist have—even one as clever as Professor Moriarty? Even so, I had no intention of letting that thought lull me into any false sense of security. There was much to be done before we pulled through. The game was afoot but it most certainly was not over.

It must have been that realisation that disturbed my sleep. I am usually a sound sleeper and, as usual, I was off the moment my head touched the pillow but then the dreams came crowding in.

I was walking through a house very like the one in Chester Square. It was totally empty of furniture and every room was mirrored, so that I could not avoid seeing my own reflection at every turn. Suddenly I heard a woman's voice crying out something and I knew it to be Alicia Creighton's. She was clearly in distress and was calling my name. I opened one door and suddenly saw her in the distance beckoning to me. She was dressed in the *Alice in Wonderland* costume and the strangest thing was that the faster I hurried towards her, the further away she seemed.

From room to room I went and each one seemed smaller than the last—or were the walls and ceiling coming towards me? Now I could catch glimpses of other people I knew scurrying past me in the opposite direction, each of them dressed as *Alice* characters.

There was Mycroft, an enormous Mock Turtle, lugubriously murmuring to himself—"Jam tomorrow and jam yesterday—but never jam today . . ."

"But that doesn't make sense," I heard my inner

voice saying—only to have Holmes, who now happened to be passing dressed as the Mad Hatter, raise his hat with the label saying "In this style—10/6d" say politely "Everything's got a moral, if only you can find it."

"That's easy enough for you to say, Holmes," I found myself thinking, "but you don't have to worry about the room shrinking." At which point Mrs. Hudson bustled past, except that she looked for all the world like the Duchess. "Soup of the evening—beautiful soup," she murmured comfortingly.

"Thank you, Mrs. Hudson—Duchess," I replied. "That sounds delicious. I just hope we get back in time for supper."

Now at last I seemed to be getting closer to Alice, which was just as well, since the rooms were not only getting smaller and smaller but darker and darker. And as I approached Alice, she seemed to change.

"But this makes no sense," I heard myself shouting.

"Take care of the sense and the sounds will take care of themselves," laughed the Alice Thing in a tone that was distinctly unpleasant. And now it seemed to turn into a large Caterpillar smoking a hookah.

"But who are *you?*" I was shouting even louder now, or so it seemed to me.

"I'm as large as life—and twice as natural," the

Caterpillar replied in what seemed an eminently reasonable tone.

"I just don't believe any of this is happening," I cried.

"If you'll believe in me—I'll believe in you," said the Caterpillar, as it slowly turned into . . . Humpty Dumpty with Moriarty's face.

"So you don't believe, eh, Doctor?" said Humpty Dumpty. "Well, I'm afraid you leave me no alternative."

I saw now that he was carefully placing a judge's black cap on top of his egg-shaped head.

"I'll be judge, I'll be jury . . . I'll try the whole case and condemn you to death. Oh, by the way, Doctor, remind me to get a bigger cap, there's a good fellow . . . there's a good fellow . . . there's a good fellow."

His moon face melted into a blur and as I struggled to bring it back into focus, it turned into Holmes. I realised that he was leaning over me and shaking me awake.

"Wake up, there's a good fellow. I need your help and we seem to have stirred up the hornets' nest right enough. I've asked Mrs. Hudson to make us a fresh pot of tea. Is there anything else that would tempt you to rise?"

"Ask her if there is any jam today?" I replied rather groggily.

Holmes laughed loudly. "Good old Watson. The fixed point in a changing world. Jam it shall be."

He went out, closing the bed-room door behind him.

When I entered the sitting room a little while later, I found Holmes deep in conversation with a tall young man of rather disreputable appearance. On my arrival, however, I was pleased to see him jump to his feet and touch his forelock. "Mornin', Doctor Watson."

Then I recognised him. "Ah, morning, Wiggins!" I replied, "and how are the Baker Street Irregulars these days?"

"Mustn't grumble, Doctor, and always better for a bit of action."

At Holmes's indication, he resumed his seat and I poured myself a much-needed cup of tea. "I've had Wiggins and his colleagues watching Chester Square for the last couple of days, Watson. Do you think you were spotted, Wiggins?"

"I'm pretty certain not, Mr. 'Olmes," the boy replied. "We took it in shifts, like. One of us would be on a delivery bike. Another would be doing some odd jobs in a neighbour's garden. Nobody ever takes notice of a young bloke like me," he added with a touch of professional pride in his voice.

Holmes looked down at a notepad on his knee.

"From the boy's description our friend has been receiving the visitors we suspected on a regular basis. Everything seemed to be proceeding in an orderly fashion until late last night. Right, Wiggins?"

"Regular 'ornets' nest it was then, Doctor. People coming and going till all hours, lights blazing and everything. Then about two-ish this one feller comes rushing in. Slicked back hair, looked like he'd seen a ghost . . ."

"Steel!" I exclaimed.

"The genuine article by the sounds of it," Holmes replied with an enigmatic glance in my direction. "And then what happened, Wiggins?"

"Well, gentlemen," said Wiggins, expansive now that he had a captive audience, "I managed to shin up a drain pipe, see, until I was next to the room where most of the noise was coming from. Then I see—saw—this Steel chap come rushing in. Two other fellers were trying to stop him but he wasn't having none of that. He goes up to where this chap Moxton is sitting at his desk and starts banging on it. And Moxton doesn't like that one bit, I can tell you."

"So then what happened, Wiggins? Be as precise as you can, if you please. A great deal may depend on it."

"Moxton just keeps staring at him and I felt all cold even where I was, I can tell you, Mr. 'Olmes. Gawd knows what it must have felt like when he was looking straight at you."

As he spoke I recalled how Holmes had once described Moriarty's unblinking reptilian gaze when angered and could well sympathise with the lad.

"Steel keeps saying as how it wasn't him, which I didn't truly understand what he meant. How could he be him and not him, if you see what I mean?"

"Perfectly. And then . . . ?"

"And then Moxton turns to 'im and says—'Steel by name but not, it would seem, by nature. I begin to wonder if you are not, after all, cast iron? And iron, my friend, is brittle. It can easily be snapped.' And then these two geezers finally get 'old of him and drag him out of the room. It was then I began to get a bit of cramp and me foot scraped on the drainpipe, see, which drew his attention. I was off out of there in no time, Mr. Holmes, I can tell you."

"You did extremely well, Wiggins. Then later this morning . . . ?"

"Buzzing like bees, they was." Winged insects seemed to loom large in the boy's vocabulary. "Packing things in vans. Me and the other lads didn't dare to get too close, in case they marked us for marking them. But I tell you, gentlemen, I could have sworn they were packed ready for somethin' like this, 'cos they were out of there in no time at all. That Moxton, 'e must have gone out the back way, cos none of us saw 'im go."

"And the lady?" I interposed.

"Never saw 'er neither, Doctor. A moonlight flit,

I'd call it—'cept it was in the daylight. And that's about it for now, I reckin."

"Well done, Wiggins," said Holmes. "Here's a little something for you and your friends. Please give them my best." And with this Holmes discreetly held out his closed hand to the young man, who palmed the offering with the practised skill of a junior Fagin. A moment later it was as if he had never been. I could see entirely why Holmes placed such faith in the services of his band of unorthodox assistants.

"So it would seem, old fellow," Holmes reflected when we were alone once more, "that we are beginning to make our presence felt. Moriarty is having to revise his plans and write friend Steel out of them. And while I do not doubt for a moment that the man can be replaced like any cog in any wheel, I do doubt that a cog of that size can be replaced in time for whatever Moriarty has in mind. With any luck we have upset his timetable and will force him into precipitate action."

"But where do you suppose he has gone—and what about Alicia?"

"Oh, someone in Moxton's position always has a valid reason for moving his base of operations around his empire. According to Lestrade's research, the house is only taken on a short term rental. As for Miss Creighton—Alicia—I must admit that young lady is beginning to cause me concern. I fear I may have made a mistake by allowing her to return there but the chance of learning something and the risk of forewarning Moriarty, I must admit, weighed heavily with me.

"Although the birds may have flown, I think it may nonetheless be to our advantage to investigate the coop. As you know, my dear fellow, it has long been my assertion that wherever any living being has passed, there must inevitably remain some mark, dent or abrasion to mark their passing—some indication that can be interpreted by the true observer. While I change, perhaps you will be so good as to bring yourself up to date with last night's reviews?" And he threw the pile of morning papers in my general direction as he left the room.

For once in a way the gentlemen of Fleet Street had found common accord. In simple terms they had turned and rent Royston Steel. Few men since Genghis Khan can have suffered such universal obloquy. Only the *Clarion* was muted and its story of "UNUSUAL DISTURBANCE IN HOUSE OF COMMONS" must have soured the professional soul even of the hacks writing to Moriarty's instruction.

Even the editorials of politically divergent publications were remarkably unanimous. The country was clearly threatened. It was time for all men of goodwill to band together and support the Government in whatever draconian action needed to be taken to root out the insidious evil in our midst. All of this in the kind of language that would have caused my friend the greatest possible displeasure, had I used it to tell one of his exploits. It was clear that Holmes had succeeded with one bold strategic stroke in diverting the force of public opinion—insofar as the newspapers were anticipating and shaping it—from the course Moriarty had so carefully set.

And there to taunt him in every agony column was the rueful countenance of the Cheshire Car. Even I had to smile when I saw it.

It was my friend's voice that tempered my pleasure. "Indeed, we have something to smile about for the first time since this affair began but we must ensure that Moriarty does not have the last laugh. His arsenal is by no means exhausted, Watson, and we must hope that we have ruffled the feathers of his pride sufficiently to lure him into breaking cover rashly. Meanwhile, I suggest we see what traces he has left for us in this particular nest . . . I despatched a note with Wiggins to ask Lestrade to meet us there with a search warrant. Much as I like to indulge your appetite for larcenous entry, old fellow, I think under the circumstances a more formal approach may be indicated."

Some few minutes later our cab was bowling into Chester Square. The scene was very different from my last visit. Instead of the procession of carriages full of revellers, the pavement outside Moxton's former residence looked distinctly deserted with scraps of paper—presumably from the hurried packing—blowing about in a chill late morning breeze. The occasional passers-by, bundled up against the winter waiting surreptitiously in the wings, went about their business unheeding and only added to the sense of desolation. The house had only been empty for a few hours but it might as well have been years.

Lestrade and two of his uniformed men were already standing by the front door, stamping their feet and blowing on their hands. Not for the first time in my observation Lestrade looked pleased to see Sherlock Holmes, although, come to think of it, his expression was perhaps more abject than pleased.

"Sorry about this, Mr. Holmes. I should have thought to have the house watched round the clock."

"I shouldn't let that worry you unduly, Lestrade," Holmes replied. "What could you have done except watch? You had no grounds to question a foreign national about his movements when you have no evidence of his wrongdoing. Had you done so, he would merely have told you that it was none of your business. No, I think we may expect to learn more about our friend's plans by his absence than by his presence. You have the warrant?"

"Just as you requested but what should I fill in on the form?"

"Oh, I think that's obvious enough. Doctor Watson and I happened to be passing and heard suspicious sounds coming from this obviously deserted house. Being good publicly-minded citizens, we immediately called the police to investigate. Isn't that so, Watson?"

"Absolutely, Holmes," I replied beginning to enjoy the way things were turning out. This was more like one of our old adventures.

"Shall we . . . ?" Holmes indicated the solid front door.

Within moments one of the uniformed constables had opened it and we found ourselves standing in that enormous main hall amid all the signs of a hasty departure. Old copies of the *Clarion* were littered around the floor and some of them looked to me as though they had been thrown down and trampled on in anger—but that could have been my fertile imagination working overtime. In the other rooms it was the same story. In every fireplace on the ground floor were the ashes from what looked like burned documents. I noticed Holmes pick up several fragments that appeared less scorched and put them away carefully in the envelope he invariably carried in an inside pocket. I knew that his bunsen burner and chemical retorts would be pressed into their odiferous service before the day was out.

The task before us was clearly enormous. At least the man who goes to find a needle in a haystack has the supposition that the haystack actually contains a needle but we had no idea what we were looking for. Eventually a short consultation resulted in the decision that Lestrade and his men should search the ground floor and the cellars, while Holmes and I would concentrate on the upper floors.

Two hours later we were none the wiser. Frankly, I was not at all sure that Holmes had expected to be, knowing the cunning mind of the man who opposed him. I reflected that I would hate to play chess against either of them with the certain knowledge that they would be mentally removing your last piece from the board before you had made your opening move.

We had started our search in Moxton's study. Like the rest of the house, it had been rented fully furnished. With the personal possessions removed it looked much as I imagine it must have looked when he moved in—with the exception of a small empty space on one wall where a picture had clearly hung.

Holmes saw my glance.

"The Greuze. Moriarty would never leave that behind. I only wonder where he kept it during his 'sabbatical'? Under the bed perhaps."

"Have you found anything, Holmes?" I asked without much hope of an encouraging answer.

150

After all, I had seen everything my friend had seen.

"Relatively little, Watson, relatively little. Other than that six men occupied one of the bedrooms as an improvised barracks. Two of them were French, two German, one almost certainly a Spaniard or Basque of distinctly peasant origin, while their leader was unquestionably our old friend, Krober. Their presence so close to Moriarty is particularly disconcerting, since they were apparently engaged in the manufacture of explosives."

"Come along, Holmes," I protested, "I passed through that same room myself and I saw nothing to lead me to those conclusions."

"That is because you were looking for obvious clues, old fellow, when the little things are infinitely the most important. Let me explain. The room is not particularly large, yet six small metal beds were crammed into it. That suggests the men in them were intended to be kept together as some sort of group. Since there was ample accommodation for them to have had a room each, they must be servants of some kind, and since Moriarty could have afforded to provide them with a degree of comfort, the deliberately spartan conditions suggest men trained to subsist—possibly in a military environment. The fact that the beds were iron cots arranged with symmetrical precision tends only to confirm that hypothesis, as do the distinctive scratch marks on the parquet floor boards."

"The Frenchmen? By the side of two of the beds were traces of ash from two *different* brands of peculiarly revolting French cigarettes and I find it unlikely that one man cooped up in this situation would have two different brands available to him—*ergo* two Frenchmen. The Spanish peasant was in the habit of sitting on the bed with his head against the wall. The type of macassar oil with which his hair was liberally doused is common in the south-west of Spain, an area which is also known for a particularly vicious type of assassin.

"The Germans, I confess, are something of a guess. Their beds were set square to the wall and showed no trace of movement. Their boots had been placed neatly at the end of the bed and the adjacent area scrupulously swept. No other race in Europe would be capable of such behaviour. I rest my case."

"And Krober?"

"Oh, the boots again. Our friend affects a boot with a curiously patterned rubber sole, designed for gripping in the wet. The marks were everywhere. Krober was clearly the leader of the group and most probably supervised the evacuation."

"Yes, of course," I muttered. "Perfectly obvious, now I come to look at it."

"All of which tells us who was here but not where they've gone."

Holmes was once again talking to himself, as he paced up and down in his impersonation of a caged tiger. "And what would they do with Miss Creighton?" The same thought had been preoccupying my thoughts since we entered the house.

"Come, Watson, let us take another look at her room."

Alicia's room was that rare combination—feminine without being fussy. I tried to look at it with Holmes's eyes. What did it tell me about its occupant?

Wherever he had taken her, Moriarty had not given her time to pack properly. In fact, my heart sank at the thought that he may not have given her time to pack at all. There were remarkably few personal possessions in the room and I felt sure that this was not because she had recently removed them. Alicia Creighton simply did not wish to leave her mark on a room that she regarded as little more than a glorified prison.

Holmes confirmed my thought process. He was standing by her open wardrobe and rifling through the clothes that were hanging there—an activity that made me feel slightly embarrassed.

"Look here, Watson, this is interesting."

At one end of the cupboard, carefully separated

from the rest were a few simple working dresses, neatly hung and pressed. "These are clearly the clothes she brought with her from her old life, while these . . ." and he indicated a number of much more expensive garments shoved higgledy-piggledy in one corner: ". . . these tell us what she felt about the finery her 'guardian' provided.

"But even more interesting is this . . ." He had closed the wardrobe and moved over to the window where a dressmaker's dummy stood dressed in the Alice costume Alicia had worn to the party. "Why did she not consign this to her pile of rejects, I wonder? Could it be because she has now begun to identify with the heroine of Moriarty's fantasy and is determined to emulate the Alice who found her way successfully through the strange imaginary universe by refusing to believe in it?"

As he spoke I found myself scanning the room. There was the dressing table with the two ebony hair brushes. I could imagine her sitting there using them on that mane of dark hair. By the mirror was a single framed photograph of a beautiful dark haired woman, obviously Alicia's mother. The face was a little drawn but the resemblance was uncanny. And then it struck me. What woman would willingly leave, even overnight, without her hair brushes and such an important personal memento?

The urgency in Holmes's voice underlined my own concern.

"Think, Watson, think! The lady knew she was in danger and she also knew that we would surely come looking for her. However suddenly Moriarty decided to decamp, she must have had time to leave some sort of clue . . ."

And then I noticed the book.

It was a battered old copy of *Alice in Wonderland* which Alicia had probably picked up at some secondhand bookstall when this Alice business had begun and she knew she had to contrive her costume. It had every reason to belong there, yet there was something about it that puzzled me. Then I realised it was the way it was placed on the dressing table. The handles of Alicia's hair brushes seemed to be angled so that they pointed to the book.

"I've got it, Holmes," I cried triumphantly, "she's left us a message in the book." It was the work of a moment to snatch it up and shake it. I fully expected to see a slip of white paper flutter to the surface of the table. Instead—nothing!

Holmes, I noticed, was running his fingers over the surface of the dressing table and now he appeared to find something. As he held it up, I saw that it was a bent hairpin that caught the light.

"Allow me," he said taking the book gently from my hand. Then, as an afterthought— "Remind me, Watson, never to take you for granted. On occasions you see straight to the heart of a problem while I am still busy defining its boundaries. Ah yes, here we have it, I believe . . ."

Now he was holding it up to the light and riffling through the pages.

"Most ingenious. Miss Creighton was too clever to commit her message to paper. Even slipped between the pages of a book, it might well be discovered. Instead she hit upon the idea of pricking out a tiny pin hole under certain words. I seem to remember seeing a pad and pencil on Moriarty's desk. Watson, if you would be so good . . . ?"

By the time I returned with the writing implements, I could tell from his expression that his intuition had proved correct.

"Take this down, Watson, if you please . . ." And he slowly began to dictate as he turned the pages. When he had finished, what I had written down was this . . .

THE KNAVE WAS STANDING . . . WITH A SOLDIER ON EACH SIDE TO GUARD HIM . . . THE JUDGE . . . WAS THE KING . . . THE KNAVE . . . TOOK QUITE AWAY! . . . INTO THE COURT . . . "YOU CAN'T SWIM, CAN YOU?" HE ADDED, TURNING TO THE KNAVE.

"What do you make of it?" I asked when I had read it back.

"Some of it is obvious enough, I think," Holmes replied. " 'The King' is clearly Moriarty who will 'judge' the prisoner who is being guarded. The 'soldiers' would seem to be the men we were discussing earlier . . ."

"And the 'Knave' . . ." I interrupted, "the Knave must be Steel. Don't you remember—at the party Steel was dressed as the Knave of Hearts?"

"Quite right, Watson, so he was. And in Lewis Carroll's story the Knave was put on trial for supposedly stealing the jam tarts. In Moriarty's book I fear Steel's crime will take on rather more significance."

"But what does the rest of it mean, in Heaven's name? The court and the swimming?"

"That is for Moriarty to know and for us to find out, I'm afraid. Miss Creighton has done wonders to leave us this much information and it is for us to fill in the blanks—and quickly, too. Certain things seem clear. Even before Tweedledum went to battle with Tweedledee, Moriarty was planning a new phase in his operation. The presence of his 'soldiers'—mercenaries would, I feel, be a better word—suggests some form of urban terrorism. A few determined and unscrupulous men, acting apparently at random, can paralyse a densely populated city at will. There have already been several such examples on the

Continent in recent months. Naturally, they made little impact on the xenophobic British press— simply those foreigners being foreign. But if they were not somehow connected, I should be very much surprised.

"Then there is the vanity factor. We have disrupted Moriarty's meticulous timetable. If I know my man, he will need to wrest back the advantage to prove that he is still in control. He will feel the need to do something highly visible and extremely destructive. It is up to us to determine precisely what in time to forestall it. And now I think we can leave any further tidying up to Lestrade and his men." He patted his pocket. "There are one or two samples here I wish to analyse . . . Explosive in nature without a doubt. If I can identify their type, dozens of our countrymen may continue to sleep soundly in their beds."

CHAPTER ELEVEN

The next two days passed more slowly than any I can ever remember. Moriarty and his men seemed to vanish from the face of the earth. Lestrade and his men—even Holmes had to admit—did a remarkable job of quartering the city and following every lead and whiff of rumour. Lestrade himself would arrive at Baker Street with monotonous regularity, his ferret face looking increasingly drawn, to report on progress—or, rather, the lack of it. Even Wiggins and his Baker Street Irregulars had nothing to report—a situation which irked those young men particularly, since they saw themselves as amateur competitors to Scotland Yard and were never so happy as when they were able to find a lead the police had missed.

The employees at the *Clarion* seemed equally and genuinely mystified. The official story was that Moxton and his entourage had taken off for an unknown European destination for an undisclosed period of time. Meanwhile, the paper was to pursue its set policies. It was a well-oiled machine that could function perfectly well without its proprietor for a few days. What appears to be the problem, gentlemen?

Amidst the frenzy of activity Holmes was, as

usual, the still centre. Shrouded in his old dressing gown he padded about the sitting room in the pursuit of various mysterious activities. Meanwhile, a stream of telegrams came and went. The information they contained appeared to confirm whatever he was thinking but I knew my friend well enough to know that none of them contained the answer to the problem that was occupying us both. In moments when he did not think himself observed I could see his brow furrowed in a frown and the lines around his nose and mouth deepen. He was too sensitive not to realise that this was one case where my professional involvement touched upon the personal.

As for myself, I was constantly reproaching myself for letting that brave young woman return to a situation all of us knew to be fraught with risk. I should have insisted, I told myself more times than I care to recall. But then I had to remind myself that this was a modern young woman—no Mrs. Pankhurst, perhaps—one who made her own decisions and lived by them.

It was late afternoon on the second day after our search of the Chester Square house and Holmes and I were sitting by the fire.

Mrs. Hudson had served us a light lunch of some cold collations, as I recall, but neither Holmes nor I had any appetite and for once Mrs. Hudson decided not to reproach us for it. His long thin fingers steepled in front of his face,

Holmes stared into the fire, as though the answer was hidden somewhere in its dancing flames. When he spoke he did not look in my direction.

"Except for the one vital piece, the puzzle is almost complete but that piece is the key to it all, Watson."

As I shifted uncomfortably in my chair, he continued: "I know how this apparent inactivity weighs upon you but we cannot afford to make a mistake now. The net is tightening around Moriarty and his accomplices and you may be sure he is well aware of the fact. The last two days have not been without some small success, old fellow. My little experiments . . ." and with a wave of his hand he indicated the array of chemical apparatus on its zinc-topped table—"even though they may offend your olfactory sensibilities, have clearly identified the substances from Moriarty's war room which, indeed, is what it was. As a result I have been able to provide Lestrade and his colleagues with enough 'ammunition'—if you will permit the pun—to apprehend certain undesirable characters in six of our larger cities."

He reached for a bundle of telegrams on the table next to him. "Let me see . . . two Frenchmen in Cardiff and Glasgow, two Prussians in Birmingham and Leeds and a particularly unsavoury Spaniard in Manchester. All of them were carrying identical explosive devices, clearly designed to create the impression of a Nihilist network at work within our midst. But perhaps the most interesting aspect of the whole business was the little experiment I urged Lestrade to try, which was to have a series of bloodhounds sniff out the presence of the explosives. When exposed to the ingredients I had in my possession, their sense of smell was unerring. Do you know, Watson, I believe I may have hit upon something here of considerable significance."

"But surely the risk of detonation . . . I mean, those poor dogs must have been in danger—and the police, too, of course." I finished lamely. But Holmes was in no mood to be bothered with trifles. "All of which makes it even more imperative for Moriarty to pull off the one big coup with which he was hoping to crown a series of smaller incidents. And it is that which we have to anticipate. Somehow I cannot bring myself to believe he will find himself able to act without using it to goad me first."

"You mean Moriarty will have to show himself again?"

"I think not, Watson. I very much believe we have seen the last of John Moxton, though certainly not the last of Moriarty. Though wearing what face?"

At that moment the telephone rang.

It was rare to see Holmes startled. It was some months since he had bowed to the march of progress and had the instrument installed but he continued to view it with a certain suspicion and rarely used it to place a call. I think he had a superstitious feeling that it might undermine the world of commonplace books, cables and the face to face consultations in which he felt at home. He glanced instinctively in my direction, as if for help, before gingerly picking up the receiver.

When he heard the voice on the other end of the wire, however, his nervousness fell away immediately. He beckoned me over and held it far enough away from his ear so that I could hear too.

There was no doubt about the identity of the speaker. It was Alicia Creighton and she was a frightened woman. She spoke hurriedly and it was obvious that she was keeping her voice low, so as not to be overheard. It gave what she said a sinister intensity.

"Mr. Holmes, thank God you're there! Did you find the book?"

Holmes spoke soothingly in an effort to calm her.

"We did, Alicia. May I compliment you on an ingenious solution. Dr. Watson is here with me. Where are you? Alicia? . . ."

There was a silence and I could imagine her perhaps going to a door to make sure that she was not being overheard. Then she continued. "We're in some place where all the windows are barred, so that I can't see out. I was brought here blindfold. There's hardly any furniture, so I'm sure he doesn't intend to stay here long. The man hates you, Mr. Holmes. He can talk about nothing else except you and whatever it is he's planning. It's soon, that's all I know, and it's big. He keeps saying the world will hear from him."

"What about Steel?" I said into the mouthpiece.

"I haven't seen him since those men took him away. I didn't like the man but he was so frightened . . . Mr. Holmes, I . . ." Her voice broke off, there was a crackle on the line, then a different voice. Moriarty's voice . . .

"Good evening, Holmes . . . Dr. Watson . . . I can almost see you sitting in front of one of Mrs. Hudson's good coal fires. You, Holmes, are wearing a dressing gown—the blue or the mouse, I wonder? I'm inclined to think the mouse, for this is certainly a two pipe problem, is it not? With any luck, three. The faithful Doctor is well into his Arcadia mixture . . ."

I put the pipe down immediately. The man had second sight.

"I wish I could describe the setting in which Miss Creighton and I are sharing this convivial conversation with you but I'm afraid that is not possible at the moment. In any case—what is Shakespeare's phrase about 'summer's lease' having all too short a time to run? We must shortly be on our way to pastures new—or at least, one of us must . . ."

164

"If you harm one hair of that woman's head, you devil . . ." I found myself shouting. Why is it that at times of stress the cliches of melodrama come first to mind? Holmes's expression helped me to control myself. He was quite right, of course. We had to keep our heads in the hope that Moriarty would let slip some clue as to his whereabouts. My outburst seemed to have amused him.

"Precisely the reaction I would expect from an officer and a gentleman, Doctor! I think I can assure you that your sentiments are greatly appreciated. Unfortunately, the lady in question is unable to come to the phone at the moment to thank you in person. But we are all busy men, gentlemen, and I'm afraid the social niceties will have to wait for another occasion—should there be one . . .

"I must congratulate you, Holmes. The passing years do not seem to have impaired your ability to be disruptive. I must admit you have caused me to, shall we say, 'adapt' my plans a little and I shall now play a slightly longer game than I had first intended. Nonetheless, our little cut and thrust once again more than compensates for a little delay.

"I had hoped to be present to both take part in and report on my own 'coronation' when the time was ripe. Now, I shall have to devise a new persona to receive that honour but receive it I shall, make no mistake about it. I hear that you have taken a few of my pawns but they are expendable. Next time I must remember to use knights or even bishops. It never does to deal at too low a level, don't you feel?

"I must say, my dear chap, I am a little disappointed in your sense of historical inevitability. I would have thought it obvious to the merest tyro that the country had reached a crisis of identity. Something is rotten not in the state of Denmark—ah, the Bard again!—but right under your noses. Change can be encouraged or—as I prefer to think—it can be forced. The country is—how can I put it?— a powder keg. All it needs is a match. But I digress . . ."

"Please continue, Moriarty," Holmes said encouragingly. "It is always intriguing to see a twisted mind at work . . ."

At that a peal of laughter chilling in its intensity, came down the phone. "Good old Holmes. The stage lost a rare actor when you committed yourself to the study of crime. Perhaps we should both have followed where Thalia and Melpomene beckoned. Who knows, we might have rivalled Irving and Tree. Which of us would have played Othello, I wonder, and which Iago?" And again the laugh. "But the Gods, it seems, willed it otherwise."

Suddenly the tone was sharper, more

businesslike. "Well, much as I have enjoyed our little chat—rather more, I fancy, than Miss Creighton here—I must attend to affairs of state. Just one last thing. You were enquiring, I believe, into the well being and whereabouts of Mr. Steel. Knowing how you like a good conundrum, Holmes, let me leave you with just one clue. Don't forget that the gentleman was—is—let's not argue tenses here—mine own invention."

And the line went dead. Strangely, the silence shrieked even louder than Moriarty's laughter.

Holmes returned the receiver to the stand as gently as if he were handling porcelain. Then he looked at me soberly.

"The damnable thing is that there is a great deal of truth in Moriarty's demented ramblings. The country very probably is living on the reputation of past glories and the widening gap between have and have-nots could easily become a political as well as a social chasm. There are vultures beyond these shores who are waiting to feast. All of this is true and, without being able to articulate it, the British people sense some of it and would like nothing more than for some latterday St. George to ride up and kill the dragon. Which is why Moriarty tried to create his own superman—his man of steel in more ways than one. His motive was cynical and self-serving but his analysis, as ever, was insightful."

"Well, you certainly dealt with that solution," I said, becoming uncomfortable with the way the conversation seemed to be tending.

"Perhaps," my friend replied, "but only temporarily. There will be others, with or without a Moriarty to prop them up. None of them will succeed for the simple reason that our society has grown too complex for a single Galahad to save it. Should such a man arise, perhaps many years from now, he will only succeed—if he does succeed—by tapping into the great heart of this great nation."

Then with a wry smile Holmes got to his feet. "Watson, you really must pull me up when I begin to wax philosophical. How many times do I have to tell you that the worst error the consulting detective can fall into is to draw conclusions without sufficient evidence?"

He began to pace the room and I knew that he was literally winding himself up to act.

"Let us address those matters we are qualified to address in the hope that such success as we may achieve will have its impact on the larger canvas. I promise you this, Watson. War in Europe may prove inevitable some day not too far distant but if it should come, it will not be by the machinations of one malignant and power crazed man called Moriarty!

"Come, old fellow," he said, throwing a pad and pencil in my general direction. "Moriarty has kindly offered us a clue but he does not know that we have—thanks to Miss Creighton—the makings of several more. If we cannot piece out their imperfections with our thoughts—Moriarty does not have a monopoly on the Bard, you see—then we are not the fellows we think we are. Now, let us set down what we have."

"Well," I said chancing my arm, "we know that Moriarty has placed Steel under house arrest, so to speak, and is holding him some-where, presumably in London. He clearly believes the man is expendable . . ."

"He 'invented' him and, therefore, believes he can destroy his own invention. 'Invented' him . . ."

"Then something about Royston going to Court," I continued, "and can he swim? Royston . . . Court . . . what's that supposed to mean?"

Holmes swung round in his chair and those piercing eyes bored into me. "Say that again, Watson."

"Say *what* again? I said about Royston going to Court . . ."

"No, you didn't, old fellow. You said 'Royston Court'. My dear fellow, I've been blind. Royston Steel has nothing to do with a Court of Law. That's simply Moriarty's little pun. 'Royston Court' is a place! And he spoke of *inventing* Steel . . . Quick, pass me my commonplace book, if you would—the one for 'S' . . ."

I did as he asked and he flicked through the well worn pages with practised skill.

"Staunton, Arthur—the forger . . . Staunton, Henry . . . hm, the man I helped to hang . . . ah, here we are—Steel, Royston . . . born, etc., etc., as I thought. Born Arthur Chadwick in Belper, Derbyshire . . . career in local politics . . . reputation as something of an orator . . . wins national debating prize which takes him to the US, where he becomes a protégé of . . ."

"John Moxton?"

"The very same, Watson, the very same. Stays in New York to work for the Moxton publishing empire and around that time changes his name to Royston Steel. Returns to England about two years ago and stands for Parliament in a marginal seat. It is generally thought that massive support from the *Clarion* swung the vote his way. The rest I think we know . . . Moriarty invented him and probably named him to symbolise the character he wished to project on the British psyche. That would account for the 'Steel'. But 'Royston' . . . ? There must be some other connection in Moriarty's empire that he is taunting us with I wonder . . ."

Throwing the commonplace book aside, he leapt to his feet and began to rummage around in another pile of books, until he emerged with a London street guide. A moment or so later—
"As I thought, it *is* a place. Watson, I am prepared

to wager you a pound of your Arcadia mixture that the answer lies in Wapping. 'Royston Court' is a location by the river, most likely one of Moriarty's hideaways. If he hasn't got Steel tucked away there, I shall be very surprised. Steel goes to Court. He could not resist the irony."

"That means he'll have Alicia there, too?"

"I think it highly likely, old fellow, but there is only one way to find out. I have a few arrangements to make first and then, as soon as is dark, we shall pay a visit to the East End."

CHAPTER TWELVE

I have often thought that Holmes demonstrated an unhealthy interest in the East End of our fair metropolis. On more than one occasion I have opened the door in Baker Street to a filthy lascar, usually sporting a livid scar down one cheek. Holmes would deny this strenuously, but I have often felt that something of the persona lingered for an hour or two even when his more familiar figure was lounging languidly in the chair opposite.

Tonight I had little to complain about. My friend was dressed as formally as if he were about to attend a society *soirée*. Catching my appraising glance, he smiled. "This is no evening for fancy dress, Watson. Our business is to unmask not to don the motley. Do you have your service revolver about you? Good. Then let us have our day in Court . . ."

The waiting carriage was soon clip-clopping its way through London's back streets towards the East End. Holmes had been adamant that we should leave our arrival until late. "On this occasion, old fellow, let darkness be our friend and give us the element of surprise. I know from my own expeditions how difficult it is to detect movement through that maze of back streets and during the daylight hours there will be too many eyes to observe and warn Moriarty of our presence."

As a result the clocks were striking their various versions of ten as we made our way through the narrow mean streets of south east London. The city itself offered its usual collection of sepia snapshots as we passed through. Young men bidding each other a tipsy "Goodnight" outside a tavern . . . elegant carriages waiting for a theatre to ring down the curtain . . . ladies of questionable origin parading under the gas lamps . . . pinched looking clerks scurrying home after an endless and poorly paid day. It was no wonder, I reflected, that Mr. Dickens had found so much material from which to weave his tales.

I became aware that the carriage had come to a halt. "The rest of the way on shanks's pony, I think, Watson," said Holmes. "If my calculations are correct, Royston Court is only a street or two from here and I made arrangements to meet— ah, here is Lestrade."

As we descended the Inspector was waiting to greet us with half a dozen uniformed constables carrying bull's-eye lanterns.

"Studied the area very thoroughly, Mr. 'Olmes, as you requested and 'Awkins here knows it like the back of his hand. Seems he was brought up in these parts."

A thin faced middle-aged constable stepped forward and respectfully touched the brim of his helmet to us.

"Mr. Holmes, Doctor Watson, an honour to be of assistance."

"Never mind that, 'Awkins, get to the point," Lestrade interrupted gruffly.

"Well, gentlemen, the locals reckon that way, way back this part of the river was considered a bit special. Lots of big houses and all the toffs going to and fro. But there was one house that they all gave a wide berth . . ."

"Royston Court," Holmes interjected, more as a comment than a question.

"That's right, Mr. Holmes," said Hawkins, clearly pleased to see Holmes living up to his reputation.

"The Roystons had arrived here from nobody knew where and built this regular mansion right on the water. Most of their visitors seemed to arrive by boat and they kept themselves pretty much to themselves. Of course, that got everybody talking from all accounts and when on certain nights strange noises were heard and lots of lights, there was talk of witchcraft and the Black Sabbath."

"Lot of stuff and nonsense, if you ask me," Lestrade snorted.

"Very likely, Lestrade," Holmes cut him off. "As Watson will tell you, I am no believer in the supernatural myself but it has often been used as an effective defence by those who—for whatever devious reasons of their own—require privacy. Pray continue, Hawkins. The concise nature of your narrative might be an object lesson to others."

I turned to see how Lestrade was taking this rebuke before I realised that Holmes was looking quizzically in *my* direction!

"It all came to a head when a woman's body was found floating off the jetty at Royston Court with some strange marks on it. The police couldn't rightly prove it had come from there but there was such a hue and cry in the local community that it wasn't long before the Roystons did a skidaddle, lock, stock and barrel. Went as sudden and secret as they arrived. And that was fifty—sixty years ago. I remember my granddad telling me the tale often enough."

"Since when, no doubt, the place has been empty. No one wanted to buy a house with possible Satanic associations, until—a year or so ago—an anonymous vendor, whom no one has ever laid eyes on, pays cash and ferries his effects in by the river entrance at dead of night. Since when, the shutters have all been drawn, no contact has been made with the outside world—which has no desire to make contact in the first place anyway."

It was amusing to see the constable's expression so closely resemble the one I had seen on countless other faces.

"But how did you know, Mr. Holmes? That's exactly what happened."

"Once one is given a piece of the puzzle and knows the designer, Hawkins, it is relatively easy to deduce the rest of the picture."

Then, turning to Lestrade—"I think you will find that the lease was taken up within days of the arrival in this country of one John Moxton."

To which Lestrade—looking like the cat who had swallowed the cream—replied—"As a matter of fact, Mr. 'Olmes, I've had the local records checked and . . ."—here he consulted his notebook—"the said property was taken on a short lease in the name of one Jabez Milverton. Now, what's so funny about that?"

And, indeed, I found it hard to understand why Holmes should have given himself over to that fit of soundless laughter that showed he was truly amused.

"One must give the devil his due," he replied, ceasing as abruptly as he had begun, "but surely you appreciate the irony, Watson? Not only has our mutual friend retained the 'J.M.' but he has made up this new identity from two of our more celebrated cases. Jabez Wilson from the affair of the spurious 'Red Headed League'—not exactly a common Christian name, I think you'll agree— and then he purloins the surname from the king of the blackmailers, Charles Augustus Milverton, the worst man in London—or perhaps I should say, the worst but one. You know, Watson, I shall be almost sorry when this affair is over. It is definitely not without its points of interest."

At that moment it came home to me what we were doing in this squalid London side street and I had a vision of a young woman in desperate need.

"Come along, Holmes," I said, perhaps more brusquely than I had intended, "this is neither the time nor the place to stand around analysing the mental aberrations of a lunatic. There is work to do." And to emphasise the point I took out and checked the mechanism of my service revolver.

"You're absolutely right, old fellow." Holmes laid a reassuring hand on my arm. "Hawkins, is there anything further to which you wish to draw our attention?"

"Well, Mr. Holmes . . ." the constable sounded diffident for the first time—"this is more hearsay, like, but a mate of mine when we were kids once claimed that he'd sneaked into the place and he said it was really creepy, like one of those houses at the fun fair. He said he couldn't wait to get out of it. Mind, he probably said that to scare us all. I remember him saying—'The people who lived there must have been mad.'"

I was the only one close enough to hear Holmes murmur to himself—" 'How do you know I'm mad?' said Alice. 'You must be,' said the Cat, 'or you wouldn't have come here.' "

Then to Lestrade—"Lestrade, post your men at every point. Watson and I will use the ground floor window. Give us five minutes, then break in the front door. The place appears empty but then appearances, as we know with this particular gentleman, can be deceptive."

Moments later we were hurrying through the swirling mist that evening had brought to the river. Every now and then I heard the hooting of the boats still plying their trade on London's great waterway, warning each other of their presence. For some strange reason I found myself thinking of mythical beasts on Loch Ness singing their siren song. How much had happened since that abortive fishing trip.

The next thing I knew Holmes had pulled me into the shadow cast by the portico of one of the strangest buildings I can remember seeing. It was as though someone had leafed through an encyclopaedia of architecture and taken details at random, then instructed a builder to assemble them as best he may. Part Georgian, part Gothic with a touch of strictly pseudo-Elizabethan, it should have been a monstrosity. As it was, intermittently shrouded with London fog, it looked splendidly eerie and almost as if it were challenging us to unlock its mysteries. It was then I noticed that it was the only house standing intact for many yards around. All the rest were derelict shells, as though the ground were contaminated.

"Moriarty is certainly assured of a degree of privacy," Holmes whispered. In the faint light of my lantern I could see that he was carefully sorting through a set of implements he had taken from an inside pocket and I recognised them as the tools of the master burglar's trade. Since he was so clearly enjoying himself, I refrained from pointing out that the mere possession of them at night was in itself a felonious offence.

As he selected a thin probe that reminded me all too forcibly of a visit to the dentist, I recalled his boasting to me on more than one occasion that he felt burglary was an alternative profession at which he would have excelled. Well, now he had the opportunity to prove it.

There was the faintest of clicks and a satisfied grunt from Holmes as a casement window swung open. A moment later we were both standing in a marble hallway that could easily have come from a Venetian Doge's palace. There was something peculiarly menacing about the very quiet and I found myself patting the pocket in which I carried my service revolver for reassurance.

The inside of the house was much bigger than it appeared from the outside. In fact, it was a veritable maze of rooms, one leading into another and each decorated—as Hawkins had predicted—

179

in a different and often bizarre style. An Egyptian room led into a Louis Quatorze suite, which became a medieval banqueting chamber. What was perfectly plain, however, was that none of them appeared to have been used for a considerable period of time. It was as though their inhabitants had been summarily recalled to their respective pages in the history book, leaving behind only an elaborate stage set.

Holmes seemed to read my thoughts. "Once again our bird has flown. I feared as much when he left us a trail to his nest. However, let us hope he has left us some chicks."

His words instantly reminded me of why we were in this place out of time and I hastened my pace, only to find Holmes's arm restraining me.

"Steady, old fellow. It seems clear that Moriarty and his men have vacated the premises for our arrival but that does not mean that the premises themselves do not contain a few surprises. In fact, I think it highly likely that the reason he was attracted to it in the first instance is that— like so many things about him—it is not what it seems.

"Do you notice something else, Watson? Although the rooms seem all of a size, in reality they are constructed with a slight curve to them. We are being led to the heart of a spiral—or perhaps a web would be a more appropriate metaphor."

He raised his head and sniffed the air which, truth to tell, was damnably musty. Whatever purpose the place served in Moriarty's scheme of things, he had made little use of it, that much was certain. There was a musty quality—and something more. As if reading my thoughts, Holmes said over his shoulder—"Black deeds have been perpetrated here, make no mistake about it. The *genius loci* never lies and this is an evil genius. Ah, yes, just as I thought."

He opened one more door and we found ourselves on a wide balcony looking down into the sunken interior of the house. There we beheld a sight that will stay with me to my dying day.

The whole of the floor some ten or twelve feet below us was also marble and laid out in squares like a giant chess board. On each of the squares, inset with some kind of glittering mosaic that made it glow in the dark, was a different symbol. Some I recognised, but others looked totally foreign. There was a goat's head, a spider, a cat and several signs that seemed vaguely astrological but about each of them there was something strangely malignant.

"The locals were apparently correct in their suspicions," Holmes said, leaning over the stone balustrade and peering into the gloom below. "Witchcraft was most certainly practised here. See the pentacle over there? Watson, be so kind as to turn up your lantern and hold it over here . . ."

As I did as he asked, I heard myself gasp, for there below us were two seated figures. The glittering symbols had sufficiently dazzled us so that only now did we see them in the flickering light of my bull's eye.

The reason we had remained unaware of their presence now became readily apparent. Both were gagged and trussed to their chairs and each was unconscious. Almost certainly drugged was my immediate thought.

Then the smaller one stirred slightly. It was Alicia Creighton! Her dark hair had been covering her face but now, as she lifted her head, it fell back and I could see those strong and distinctive features. She appeared unhurt but her face was drawn. I called her name but Holmes, as ever the voice of reason, quietly said what was going through my mind.

"I doubt if she can hear you, old fellow. Moriarty has certainly sedated them in expectation of our arrival. I think we have more cause to be concerned about her companion. He looks to be in a bad way to me."

Now I could recognise the other figure as Steel—and what a strange figure he made. He was dressed in the costume he had worn at Moxton's fancy dress party but this Jack or Knave of Hearts was no longer the elegant man about town. The costume was crumpled and begrimed and the face pinched and unshaven. It was clear the man had suffered greatly during the last few days. Whatever mistakes he had made, I had no wish to see him degraded in this way.

"Holmes, we must do something," I cried, "we can't let them stay there another moment." And with that I made to climb over the balcony, even though the drop to the marble floor was a dangerous one. It was something in Holmes's voice that made me stop.

"Indeed, Watson, and so we shall but first we must ascertain precisely what. Why do you think Moriarty pointed our feet in this direction? He expects us to be standing on this very spot. How ironic if we were to prove to be the executioners of his prisoners!"

My friend's words were like a dash of cold water. Of course, he was right. Immediately I began to use the lantern to examine what could be seen of the rest of the hall. As I did so, I heard a faint murmur.

"Did you say something, Holmes?"

But, as I looked round, I saw him raise a finger to his lips. His brows were drawn together into hard lines and those sharp grey eyes were focused like none I have ever seen in another human being. He was straining to hear the sounds that were coming from Steel.

The man was not fully conscious and I could swear that he was not aware of our presence. Whatever he was trying to impart was something that was possessing him. I leaned forward in unconscious imitation of Holmes's posture and heard what sounded like—"Not a Court but a House . . . not a Pack but a House."

Now, as I leaned further forward, the light from the lantern played on Steel's face and I saw the most surprising thing. He was wearing one of those false beards and moustaches that are commonly sold by theatrical costumiers. Someone had obviously hooked it on to him after settling him in the chair and his struggles, feeble though they may have been, had caused it to slip to one side, giving him what should have been a faintly ridiculous air—an air that ought to have been compounded by the tall felt hat with a rakish plume that had been jammed on to his head. Instead, the effect was unsettling, as though the man were shedding one identity and assuming another before our eyes.

Suddenly I heard a crashing noise from somewhere at the back of the house and Holmes sprang forward with a cry.

"Lestrade! What was I thinking of? We must stop him, Watson, before it is too late."

"Too late for what?" I shouted as I followed him through the maze of rooms back to the hallway by which we had gained access to this house of illusion. In seconds we passed through cultures and centuries, as room gave way to room.

"I very much fear that Moriarty has set the spring which, through my blockheadedness, is about to be sprung."

We were now literally running and I cursed my own lack of fitness. Ahead of me Holmes burst into the entrance hall, where Lestrade and half a dozen uniformed men were now pushing through the wreckage that had been the front door of Royston Court.

"Lestrade! You must not . . ."

Holmes shouted but Lestrade put up a patronising hand before my friend could reach him. "Don't you worry now, Mr. 'Olmes. Scotland Yard is here to take care of things."

Now I saw what Holmes and I had both missed in the gloom. Opposite the open front door, but slightly to one side of it and now clearly illuminated by the lights from the street outside, and the lanterns of Lestrade's men, was another door. My sense of the geography of the place told me that it had to lead into what I had by now classified as the Satanic Chamber. Even as he spoke, two of Lestrade's burlier men took a run at the door, which gave way at the impact of sturdy official shoulders.

By this time I had caught up with Holmes and heard his defeated sigh as the room was suddenly revealed in all its barbaric splendour. There was Alicia and—heaven be praised—she was beginning to stir. There was Steel and again the sight of him brought a flash of memory that was gone almost before it registered.

I heard Lestrade say—"Hello, what 'ave we here?"—and then, in front of our eyes, Steel disappeared. The ground beneath him literally opened up and swallowed him.

There was absolute silence. The look on Lestrade's face as it turned in our direction was a picture to behold. "But Mr. 'Olmes . . ."

"I think you will find a mechanism linking the opening of the main doors of the room with a trapdoor under the square on which our friend Steel was carefully placed. As you will notice, freed of his weight, it has now returned to its original position. Don't blame yourself unduly, Lestrade. We were not meant to take him alive, so that he could tell us his side of the story. If you had not triggered it, one of us most certainly would have. Unless I am very much mistaken, the main sewer runs directly under this house into the river. I doubt we shall see the poor devil again until the tides see fit to return him to us."

"But what about Alicia—Miss Creighton?" I said for Lestrade's benefit.

In answer Holmes walked straight into the room and across the arcane mosaics until he was by Alicia's side.

"What are you doing, Holmes?" I shouted, expecting to see the ground open up beneath them at any second.

"Don't worry, old fellow." Holmes was almost amused at my display of concern. "This kind of mechanism is employed for a specific purpose and that purpose has been accomplished. Notice where Steel was sitting. In relation to the other symbols he was in the *locus* of the satanic sacrifice. It would be most unlikely the room would be equipped for more than one. And now, as I see Miss Creighton seems to be recovering consciousness and, as you are the one with the medical qualifications, I believe this is your department."

Before he had finished speaking I was at Alicia's side and unfastening the ropes that bound her to the chair. Moments later I had carried her to what I still considered the relative safety of the main hallway and placed her on one of the few chairs. By now her eyelids were fluttering and when her eyes finally did open, I was glad to be the first person she saw.

"John," she said and her hand gripped mine. "I knew the two of you would find me . . ." She forced a smile, "I just wasn't sure you'd find me alive."

Then some memory of the recent horrors seemed to seize her and her grip on my hand tightened.

"It was a nightmare," she said, her eyes widening but unseeing, as she looked into that second Chamber of Horrors we had seen in recent days. "He still looked like Moxton but it was if you were seeing someone else emerge who had been using his body."

There was no need to ask whom she meant by "he".

"He knew I'd been to see you and Mr. Holmes and he guessed why. Don't ask me how he knew—but he knew. From that moment his manner towards me changed completely and he had me watched. If I wanted to go out for a walk, he'd have one of those strange foreign men accompany me. He said it was for my protection. The town was not safe with all these terrorists about. At one point I lost my temper and said his men were more than enough to terrorise any terrorist. But he just laughed a horrible cold laugh and said he must protect his 'investment', I think he called it. I was a prisoner, that's all there was to it."

"And what about Steel?" I asked, while I tried to chafe some warmth back into those little hands.

"Something terrible seemed to happen to change everything," she went on. "Last night I was awakened by a terrible commotion. Doors banging. Men shouting and cursing. Most of the excitement seemed to be centered around his study. I crept out of my room. For the last several days he'd left a man on guard in the corridor but whatever was happening had obviously

188

distracted him. I was able to get close enough to listen through the door that someone had left ajar."

The memory of it all seemed to agitate her afresh and I tried to tell her that there was plenty of time to tell her story later but she would have none of it.

"No, no, don't you see, John, I may know something or have heard something that you and Mr. Holmes need to know—something I may not even be aware of?"

Calming herself, she continued. "I could hear that one of the voices was Steel's. At first he seemed angry and seemed to be pounding the table."

She was describing precisely the scene young Wiggins had spied on from the window.

"But then Moxton—or Moriarty or whoever that devil is—began to speak. He spoke in a cold hard voice that was too soft for me to hear but what-ever he said, it reduced Steel to silence. I risked a quick look through the crack of the door and I swear he was shivering. Then I heard Moxton say something about iron being brittle. Just then there was a noise at the window."

Exit Wiggins, I thought to myself.

"When Moxton returned from the window, one of his men must have asked him what caused the noise. 'Oh, nothing but a rat in the arras,' he replied with that horrible cold laugh again. Then he said something which frightened me even more. 'My dear Steel,' he said, 'I'm afraid you are becoming something of a trial to me. Which means that I have no alternative but to put *you* on trial. And since Mr. Carroll has proved such a helpful guide to our recent actions, would it not be fitting to take one more leaf out of his book, hm? Let me see, now, how did *his* trial scene play? Ah yes, "Sentence first—verdict afterwards." So much tidier, don't you agree?' Then he said 'Hold him!' to one of his men and there was a brief scuffle. Then he went on—and I swear to you, John, I had this mental picture of a horrible little boy—a horrible *clever* little boy—pulling the wings off flies. He said—'I'm afraid the jury have come to the unanimous conclusion that you are guilty, my dear fellow. Such a pity but the voice of the people must be heard in the land. And speaking of voices, I'm sure that, were you not to have that rather unsavoury gag in your mouth, you would now be asking me what your punishment was to be . . .' "

It was then I realised that Holmes had now returned and must have heard most of the recent account.

"Go on—Alicia, I beg you. And what was the punishment to be?"

"That *was* the strangest thing, Mr. Holmes. It made no sense at all. Moxton laughed again and said—'I'm afraid your next role is to be what our American cousins quaintly call the "fall guy" . . .' And that's all I heard. They all started moving towards the door. I think they were dragging Steel. I ran back to my room . . ."

Suddenly my not very nimble brain began to race. Images like the fragments in a kaleidoscope came together and separated, came together and separated. I heard Alicia ask Holmes if this terrible business was finally over and Holmes's reply that he feared Moriarty had one more card to play. But all of this seemed to be happening a long way away.

Then the pieces stopped circling and came to rest. I saw a picture in my mind that could not have been clearer. It was of the dummy I had meant to study more closely at Madame Tussaud's. The man was wearing medieval costume complete with plumed hat. For some reason he was carrying a piece of cardboard in front of him and now I could see that it had a drawing on it. Roughly sketched, as if by the hand of a mischievous child, was the smiling face of a cat . . .

In the far distance I heard Holmes say—"Just *which* card that is we now have to determine . . ."

And, as if from the bottom of a well, I heard myself say—"I think *I* can tell you that . . ."

CHAPTER THIRTEEN

I cannot ever remember being the centre of attention as I was at that moment. No one asked a question. Their eyes spoke for them.

To this day I cannot explain what made it happen. Heaven knows, I am not by nature an intuitive man. But suddenly several pieces fell together in my mind and formed a pattern that made sense.

It was Holmes who triggered it when he talked of Moriarty having one more card to play. And then I saw Steel in that tattered Knave of Hearts costume and heard his last demented babbling—"Not a Court but a House . . . Not a *Pack* but a *House*." It had made no sense at the time but now I found myself thinking of the Court scene ending of *Alice in Wonderland*, when Alice cries "You're nothing but a pack of cards!" just before she wakes up.

Not a *Pack* but a *House of Cards* . . . something insubstantial, something ready to fall. And then the strange hat and beard Steel was wearing. I'd seen them before—and recently, too. But where?

Click went the last piece. The dummy I'd hurried past in the Chamber of Horrors without stopping to read the legend the bearded man in the plumed hat had been given to carry.

192

"Moriarty is going to blow up the Houses of Parliament," I said as calmly as I knew how.

"Of *course*—The country is a powder keg and all it needs is a match. And the 'fall guy' is—*Guy Fawkes!*" Holmes exclaimed. "Watson, if ever I appear to you to be arrogant in the future, I implore you to remind me of this moment of my abject humiliation. *I* saw but I did not observe. You and you alone were the lightning conductor."

Alicia said nothing but I felt a gentle hand on my sleeve and the look in her eyes was one I had not seen since my dear Mary Morstan all those years ago.

Holmes now called Lestrade over to join us and succinctly communicated what we had now learned.

"It may well be Moriarty's one fatal weakness that, once he has devised a scheme, he is loath to change it, for to do so would admit the successful intervention of another mind. The same vanity that obliges him to leave us these clues also convinces him that we shall be unable to follow them to a successful conclusion—or at least, not in time. To that degree I can sympathise with the workings of that devious mind. To live on the edge is the only true excitement in life."

"So you reckon he's serious, Mr. 'Olmes?" Lestrade scratched his head at the immensity of the thought.

"Deadly serious, Lestrade. Just consider the

pattern as it has evolved. All the earlier disruptions were somehow connected with Parliament. The white rabbits, the Foreign Secretary, the Home Secretary . . . Steel, the would-be King Across the Water. Which is why it was particularly galling for Moriarty when I employed the same medium to subvert him.

"He knows full well that anything that happens in the Mother of Parliaments will not only focus the eyes of the world but undermine confidence, both at home and abroad, in the stability of this country. To repeat the attempt and succeed where Guy Fawkes failed would be the culmination of his present plans. Without Watson's brilliant deduction, he might well have pulled it off . . ."

"Nothing, really," I muttered, feeling myself blush like a schoolgirl. "Lucky guess." Praise from Holmes comes so rarely that I have never learned how to handle it in public. My friend was not known to be generous when it came to acknowledging the contributions of others.

"Well," said Lestrade, "there's one good thing . . ."

"And what might that be?" Holmes enquired with a dangerous calm in his voice.

"We've got plenty of time to nip the Professor's little plan nicely in the bud. Unless I'm mistaken, Mr. Fawkes tried his little bit of fun and games on November the Fifth. Today's only the Fourth."

"Once again I must beg leave to question your conclusion, Lestrade. I think you will find that the history books record that Fawkes and his fellow conspirators planned to detonate their barrels of gunpowder soon after midnight when November the Fourth had just turned into the Fifth. I see by the watch you insist on waving about so aimlessly that the time is now just after eleven o'clock. We may have barely an hour to bring this matter to a safe conclusion. I suggest . . ."

At that moment there was a series of staccato explosions, rather like fire crackers going off. The next thing I knew snakes of flame were crawling up the tapestry-covered walls of the Satanic Room. Being old and desiccated, the tapestries burned like tinder and the result was soon a vision from Hell, as the faces of demons and goblins appeared to rise from the fire before being consumed by it. Ashes and tendrils of burning fabric started to shower on to the marble floor below, casting a flickering light on the occult symbols embedded there. The sight was so phantasmagoric as to be almost beautiful and we all stood there transfixed—except Holmes, who seized Alicia and me by the arm and hurried us to where the broken door stood ajar.

"Quick. There's not a moment to lose. Gunpowder, treason and now plot. The cunning devil has set explosive devices on a timer. No doubt the breaking of the door triggered it. Moriarty hoped to destroy the evidence and us with it."

As we emerged into the courtyard beyond, we heard another series of explosions, louder than the first, from all over the house. There was the sound of glass breaking as windows exploded and we were all showered with flying shards before we reached the comparative safety of the street.

Turning to look at Royston Court, now with streams of fire flickering from every window like obscene tongues, I found myself shivering, although the night was not particularly cold. Can a building take on the quality of evil through the nature of those who built it and from the sinful purpose for which they used it? If it could, then this one did. I seemed to still hear the house spitting defiance until we were safe in our carriage and the sound of the approaching fire engines drowned it out.

When we were well out of the vicinity, Holmes ordered the driver to stop and went back to the carriages that held Lestrade and his men. I could see them engaged in earnest conversation and then the smaller and faster of the carriages took off at a great pace in the general direction of Whitehall.

Alicia and I were left alone in the four-wheeler. On leaving the house I had insisted on draping my ulster around her and now, as she sat back, she looked for all the world like a small child cocooned against all harm. She looked at me for a moment in silence, then reached out and took my hand.

"John H. Watson," she said simply. "Thank you. There are no words for what you and your friend have done and, even if I could find them, neither of you would wish to hear them. So, may I thank *you* on behalf of you both?"

And with that, she leaned forward and kissed me on the cheek. Now I was the one who had no words.

I was saved from the necessity of speech by Holmes's return. Those grey eyes missed nothing, of that I am sure, but he merely said: "Time is of the essence, I'm afraid, old fellow. I have arranged for one of Lestrade's men to take—Alicia—back to Baker Street into Mrs. Hudson's good care."

Then to his surprise as well as my own, I heard Alicia say—"Mr. Holmes, if you imagine for one moment that, after all I have been through, I intend to be consigned to the category of 'Women and Children' when this little drama reaches its climax, then your knowledge of the modern woman is sadly incomplete. You say that time is of the essence. Then I suggest we waste no more of it. Driver, the Houses of Parliament!"

Holmes was hard put to it to swing himself up into the carriage before the driver cracked his whip and we were on our way. I stole a glance in his direction and the play of emotions across that finely drawn face would have made a narrative in itself. Nonetheless, I would have taken a bet that the dominant expression was one of amused satisfaction. His quick glance in my direction told me that I must have been smiling.

A few moments later he explained his plan.

One of Lestrade's men had been sent ahead to dig Mycroft out of the depths of the Diogenes Club and have him meet us close to Westminster Abbey. Even with the House sitting, his authority would take us anywhere within the complex of buildings that made up the seat of Government, but it was important we rendezvous out of sight of Moriarty's agents, who would certainly have set up a surveillance.

"I need hardly add that we must proceed with extreme caution. The charges are undoubtedly set already and we have just seen at Royston Court how effectively they work. Tonight's debate will find some six hundred people in the Chamber immediately above and, if this morning's newspapers are correct in their surmise, several European dignitaries are to be present as guests and observers. The subject of the debate is somewhat ironic, in the light of recent events. It deals with greater European collaboration against the threat of terrorism."

With that he sat back, pulled his hat down over his eyes and appeared to go to sleep.

As the carriage clip-clopped briskly through the south London streets I looked down at the young woman sitting between us. She, too, was sleeping and her dark head had fallen on my shoulder. Why was it that, in the midst of all the terrible events unfolding around us, I wanted nothing more than to keep her safe from harm? Was there something about the line of the jaw or the curve of the lip that brought back memories of my own dear Mary and a marriage death cut all too short? Was some force outside us all trying to tell me that grief must give way to a new life in the great scheme of things? All of these speculations and more were running round in my brain as we drew up in the shadow of Westminster Abbey, a moonlit stone's throw from the Mother of Parliaments. As if to remind us of its presence, Big Ben struck the three-quarters of the hour. A mere fifteen short minutes separated us from Moriarty's devilish *dénouement*.

For a man who had supposedly been sound asleep, Holmes leapt to the ground with remark-able agility, leaving Alicia and I to make our own way over to the group huddled over a map dwarfed by Mycroft's huge hands. As we joined them, he was explaining something to Holmes and several of Lestrade's men. I noticed Hawkins among them.

"Here, here and here . . ." and his finger stabbed various locations on the map—"are the various entrances for the staff."

Hawkins nodded. "We have our men covering

all of them. Go on, sir, I expect the Inspector will be here any minute."

"Now this . . ." the finger hovered—"is the entrance to the Main Lobby. All visitors come and go through here. With all of this I think I may say I am tolerably familiar. As far as the nether regions of the building are concerned, I regret to say they are a closed book. However, I am reliably informed that this . . ."—the finger stabbed once more—"is the door leading to the cellars and it is kept locked at all times when the House is in session. Of course, in a building of this age with all the many additions, I very much doubt if anyone truly knows all the nooks and crannies."

"Take my word, one man has made it his business to know them by now," Holmes interjected. "Gentlemen, we do not have a moment to waste, yet we must so dispose ourselves that we do not create alarm. The first sign of an attempted evacuation will undoubtedly cause Moriarty to act precipitately.

"Mycroft, I know, will not take it amiss if I say that, once we have effected our entry to the Lobby, his task is to watch, wait and protect our backs—not least from official interference. We have no time to fill out official forms or argue protocol. You catch my drift, Mycroft?"

"My dear brother, it will be my pleasure to bind officialdom hand and foot in its own red tape, should the occasion arise. Gentlemen, shall we . . .

"I beg your pardon, I should also say '. . . and Lady' . . ."

"Surely Alicia . . ." I began to object but Holmes intervened. "With Moriarty's men undoubtedly roaming the area, I am more inclined to think the young lady will be safer in our company than out of it, old fellow." A quick nod from Alicia showed that his plan had at least one firm supporter.

In twos and threes we made our apparently casual way across the road towards the Houses of Parliament. Because of the importance of this emergency debate, there was a steady stream of people passing to and fro, so that we did not appear particularly conspicuous as we passed through those historic portals.

Holmes, Alicia and I formed one group, talking animatedly and pointedly looking around us at the architectural splendours, for all the world like tourists seeing the sights for the first time. Hawkins and two other plain clothes constables made their way to the notice boards and loitered with noticeable intent to check something or other on them, while carefully scanning the area.

Mycroft, having nodded us all past the uniformed officials on the door, was on the point of leading the way unobtrusively in the direction of the cellar door when he was seized upon by a passing dignitary whose name was a household word.

"My dear Mycroft. The very fellow we need to

settle an argument . . ." And the next moment the elder Holmes was in the middle of a small knot of grand and reverend seigneurs. The raised eyebrow turned in our direction said more than words that even he could not brush aside this particular company with impunity. We must proceed alone.

No sooner had he observed his brother's distress signals than Holmes gripped us both by the arm.

"Quickly, old fellow. By my calculations we have precisely seven minutes. If memory serves, Mycroft's map has the door to the cellars at the end of that corridor . . ."

All pretence of being tourists gone, the three of us hastened across the echoing hall and were soon alone in a short passage way. Behind us the bustle of the place we had just left was now a low-pitched hum and we could hear our own footfalls echo on the stone floor.

"A few yards further on the left, I think," said Holmes, consulting the folded map he had pulled from his pocket.

It was then that I saw Lestrade. He suddenly appeared from behind one of the many ornate pillars that broke up the expanse of wall. In the dim light in this little used annex it was difficult to see his expression but his body language was clear, as he raised a hand in greeting.

"Lestrade," I cried as we drew nearer, "what have you found?"

"False alarm, gentlemen, I'm glad to say. Miss

Creighton . . ." and he touched the brim of his bowler in salutation. I thought it a little strange that he didn't raise it to a lady but the thought didn't really register in the heat of the moment. Instead I almost shouted in relief—"False alarm?"

"That's right, Doctor. Seems like the Professor was having one of his little jokes at our expense. I've been all round down there with my boys and everything is tickety-boo. Looks like we'll have to think again. Well, if you'll excuse me, Mr. 'Olmes—Doctor, I'll just tell me boys they can call it a night. Why don't I pop round to Baker Street first thing in the morning and we can have a powwow . . . ?"

"Excellent work, Lestrade," Holmes interrupted enthusiastically. "By the way, I must congratulate you on the work of that young constable we met earlier, Hawkshaw?"

I was about to say—"Surely you remember the man's name was *Hawkins*—not Hawkshaw?"—when I heard Lestrade say—"One of our very finest, Hawkshaw. He'll be glad you appreciated his efforts."

"I'm sure he will. Except that 'young' Hawkshaw's name is Hawkins and he's not a day under fifty. And you, Lestrade, I see have taken to wearing an overcoat at least two sizes too small for you and buttoning it all the way up—a practice you have singularly failed to observe in all the years I have known you. Furthermore, I have never yet heard you to refer to your associates as anything but your 'men'—never your 'boys'. I have only one question for you, Moriarty—what have you done with Lestrade?"

I felt Alicia stiffen at my side. I could well understand that she must be feeling that she was condemned to be part of a circle that would never be broken. At literally the eleventh hour were we doomed to be back where we started?

"I see your legendary powers have not deserted you, my friend, but frankly, I had hoped for something a little more subtle. A coat cuff brushed the wrong way. A vocal inflexion misplaced by a few miles from the good Inspector's 'patch'— Hoxton, if I'm not mistaken? Really, Holmes, in my academic days I would have been hard pressed to give you more than a Beta plus."

"I shall be happy to settle for a Beta on this occasion, Professor, if that is the price of putting you where you belong," Holmes replied calmly. "Watson, perhaps you would be good enough to retrace your steps and bring 'young Hawkins' to do what is necessary?"

Fool that I was, I had failed to notice that, as he spun his web of words, Moriarty had gradually moved nearer to us. Now, as Holmes broke his concentration long enough to glance in my direction, Moriarty threw an arm around Alicia and, drawing a pistol from his pocket, used her as a human shield. Slowly he began backing them both away towards a door in the wall behind him.

I began to draw my own service revolver, only to have Moriarty wave his own in my direction.

"The hero is a tempting part to play, Doctor, but I somehow doubt that a dead Boswell would be able to do justice to his friend's exploits—always supposing there are clients who will wish to do business with someone who is seen to have failed as signally as Mr. Sherlock Holmes."

At which point a voice behind us said—"Mr. Holmes? Mr. Sherlock Holmes? Is there something I can do to help?"

I turned instinctively to find a young man approaching us, clearly under the impression that we had lost our way. He was fresh faced with an almost baby-like complexion and thinning fair hair and I wasn't sure whether to bless or curse him for his intrusion.

My mind was made up for me a moment later, when I heard the solid thud of a door closing and I turned to find Holmes and I were alone in the corridor. Moriarty and his hostage were gone.

Holmes ran to the door and tried the handle. It was firmly locked and barred from the inside and it was equally clear that none of my friend's picklocks was likely to make an impression on it. By this time the young man was at our side and seemed to be immediately aware that his intervention had complicated rather than eased matters. Instead of asking for an explanation or offering an apology, he looked Holmes squarely in the eye in a way I have seen few men do and said simply—"I spend a lot of time in this place and one day I hope to spend rather more. The one advantage is that I do know the ins and outs of it pretty well. Would it interest you to see the service entrance, Mr. Holmes?"

"It most certainly would," I said, speaking for both of us. "Lead on!"

Sensing our urgency, he sprinted down the corridor with us in close pursuit until he came to a narrow side passage containing nothing but a small door with its paint peeling. It was obvious that no one of consequence was expected to penetrate this far into the entrails of the House. At first the handle refused to turn and my heart sank. Then, with a strength that belied his slender frame, our new friend put his shoulder to it and with a complaining screech, it opened inwards, revealing a dimly-lit corridor.

We immediately flattened ourselves against the wall on either side of the aperture. For all we knew we might walk into a fusillade of bullets but nothing disturbed the silence that greeted us. Putting his finger to his lips, Holmes edged his way around the door frame until he stood in the passage way beyond. Only then did he beckon the two of us to join him.

The passage was quite empty in both directions and then our young friend pointed to the left. As he did so, I could begin to make out the rumble of mens' voices some way ahead. Slowly we inched our way along in the gloom. Whatever purpose the place had served in the past, it was no longer in active service. We passed empty shelves strewn with cobwebs and our companion whispered in my ear—"Looks like it hasn't been used since Guy Fawkes's time."

Holmes beckoned me to his side. "Do you have your service revolver ready, Watson? Good man. Let us hope your eye has not lost the sharpness it had at Maiwand. I fear this can only end badly."

We came to a turn in the passage and peered around it gingerly. Directly ahead of us was what was obviously the Main Cellar. There two men— one of whom I recognised as Krober—were bent over a mechanical contraption not unlike the one Holmes and I had seen up at Loch Ness. Wires led off it to a series of packages I could see were fastened to the foundations of the building.

"The explosives!" I breathed to Holmes. He barely nodded. "Enough to blow up this building and everyone in it."

Krober was now unrolling a thicker cable and backing along another passage way similar to the one we were in. "They will take that to their point of exit and detonate the explosion from there."

"But where's Moriarty?" I hissed.

The question was answered for me, as the Professor stepped out of the shadows next to where Krober had been standing, his arm still encircling a struggling Alicia. Every instinct in me told me to rush at the man and engage him hand to hand but Holmes pointed soundlessly at the revolver still held tightly in Moriarty's free hand. Long before I reached him he could easily have picked me off and Alicia, too, for that matter. I had no delusions as to what the man was capable of, if pressed.

I turned to my old friend. If we had been in tighter corners, I could not for the life of me remember what they might have been.

"What are we to do, Holmes?"

"I think it is time we called in reinforcements, old fellow."

"Reinforcements? What reinforcements? No one else knows we are here."

"Watson," Holmes murmured almost under his breath, "how often must I remind you of my old maxim that, when you have eliminated the impossible, whatever remains, however improbable, must be the truth. And Truth, said Jesting Pilate . . ."

With that he raised his voice and called out— "This way, men. Over here and the rest of you cover the other exits!"

I was rendered speechless by his effrontery but, to his undying credit, our new young friend picked up the thread immediately and cried— "Right behind you, Mr. Holmes . . . come on, lads. Rogers, Harris, you take that way . . ."

The effect on Moriarty's men was instantaneous. They dropped the cable as if it were red hot and scuttled off down the far corridor, leaving Moriarty alone but far from finished. Raising his revolver and maintaining his grip on Alicia, he pointed it unwaveringly at the nearest barrel of explosive.

"A neat trick, Holmes, but I'm afraid it won't work. One bullet and the whole place will blow sky high. Personally, I've always enjoyed playing for high stakes but I wonder whether you feel you have the right to risk so many lives on a bluff? Miss Creighton and I are going to take a little walk and if any of you try to follow us, I should perhaps remind you that I am an expert shot and a barrel is—how shall I put it?—a sitting target. *A bientôt*, gentlemen."

As he began inching backwards down the passage his companions had used I fingered my service revolver, trying to decide whether I could get off a clean shot. Fear of hitting Alicia was balanced by the thought that I might well cause Moriarty to fire instinctively into the explosives. While I remained indecisive the man was getting away from us!

Then out of the corner of my eye I sensed a rapid movement. I turned to see the young man running straight at Moriarty and his prisoner. The manoeuvre was so unexpected that Moriarty was momentarily nonplussed. And then Alicia played a master stroke that only a woman could think of. Twisting in her captor's grip, she screamed into his face with all her might. I could see Moriarty flinch at the noise and at that very moment our young friend threw himself bodily at Alicia in a sort of improvised rugby tackle and bore her to the ground out of Moriarty's arms, leaving him standing there disoriented and temporarily defenceless.

I heard Holmes cry—"*Now,* Watson!" and I loosed off a couple of rounds, one of which took Moriarty in the shoulder, causing him to drop his gun. Before I had the chance to fire again, he had spun on his heel and disappeared into the darkness of the passage behind him.

"Give me your revolver, old fellow, and look after Alicia and the young man. I must finish this alone." And with that Holmes began to run down the passage after his old nemesis.

By the time I reached them they were both on their feet, shaken but apparently little the worse for their ordeal. The first thing I did was to shake Alicia's saviour warmly by the hand. "That was one of the bravest acts I've seen on the battle field or off it," I said. "I'd like to think I'd have had the presence of mind—let alone the courage—to do the same at your age but I'm not so sure that I would."

"I know you would, John," said Alicia, reasserting a woman's true priorities by doing her best to rearrange a dress that was looking distinctly the worse for wear, "I have not the slightest doubt about it." Which made me feel distinctly better.

Our mutual admiration society was cut short by two other gun shots echoing back down the corridor. Without exchanging another word, we all three began to run.

How far we ran I have no idea. Like the corridors in *Alice* this one seemed endless. Around the corners, down steps and through doors that had been left ajar we ran. We passed the discarded cable Moriarty's men had flung aside in their flight. At one point we came across the surrealistic sight of Lestrade's coat and bowler hat. By the accident of the way they had fallen, it looked as though the Inspector had fallen face forward on the ground and then somehow deflated.

At regular intervals there were splashes of blood, confirming my feeling that at least one of my bullets had found its mark. But what of the other shots we had heard? Did the Professor have another weapon? Had his associates waited and had Holmes found himself in an ambush? Were the Houses of Parliament to be a substitute for the Reichenbach Falls?

We burst out of this seemingly endless corridor through one last door and found ourselves on a river walkway. There was the great city, bathed in moonlight, going about its nocturnal business quite unaware of how close it had been to disaster. It was a vista fit for the brush of a Turner but I had eyes only for the tall figure poised on the river wall and looking down into the dark water below.

"Holmes," I cried, "thank God you're safe!" A moment later we were all at his side, as he climbed down to the safety of the path.

"Yes, old fellow, safe to fight another day. Though let us hope this particular battle is over at last."

Then he told us of the events that had taken place after that pursuit beneath the seat of Government.

"As I have mentioned to you more than once in the past, old fellow, I have often observed that there is a perverse streak in the greatest criminals, amounting almost to a need to be caught. They are almost begging for someone to put an end to their crimes. And as Moriarty and I were alone in that dark passage way, I had the strongest sense that it scarcely mattered which of us was in pursuit of the other. We were locked, as ever, in some pre-determined struggle over which neither of us had any control and the whole outcome was somehow already determined. There must come a time when the fox wishes to be caught and the whole bloody business over with. Until then it is forced to run and run."

"And what happened to the fox?" I asked gently, for I could sense he was in a strange and highly charged mood.

"It was the most curious thing, Watson," he replied pensively. "I burst out of that door just as you did, having seen the trail of blood along the way. And then I saw him. Realising that the path led nowhere but to those iron gates which, in his weakened condition, he could not possibly scale, he had climbed on to the parapet where you found me . . ."

He indicated the spot. In my mind's eye I could see that baleful figure, backlit by the lights of the metropolis, clutching his shoulder but still dignified in defeat.

"'Come, Holmes,'" my friend was speaking again and I could hear the voice of Moriarty, "'surely you are enough of a gentleman to administer the *coup de grâce*?' I raised your revolver—the revolver I have so often bidden you carry—and fired—twice. But I freely confess I could not bring myself to fire at him. Then, as if on cue, Big Ben began to toll midnight. He stood there for a moment longer and then he said quietly, almost sadly—'The question is which is to be master—that's all. Humpty Dumpty, Holmes—Humpty Dumpty.' Then he seemed to let himself fall. By the time I reached the spot there was no sign of him."

"Humpty Dumpty had a great fall . . ."

It was our young friend speaking the words that were in all our minds. Alicia looked down into the dark swirling waters carried in on the evening tide. "And I doubt whether all the King's horses and all the King's men could put him together again."

I looked at the four of us, as bedraggled a bunch as one could hope to see this side of Limehouse. We had survived so much these past few hours and now, when we had so much in which to rejoice, we stood there with a distinct air of anti-climax in the air.

"Well, Holmes," I said with an air of forced jolity, "you've settled the oldest score of all." My friend looked at me sombrely.

"So I have, old fellow, so I have."

Then, like a host at a party suddenly remembering his manners, he turned to our young friend, who looked as though he were ready to embark on the whole affair all over again, and said quietly—"And you, sir, we are greatly in your debt. If ever you are in need, Sherlock Holmes and Doctor Watson will be at your service."

"Indeed, indeed," I added heartily. "But my dear fellow, we don't even know your name?"

The young man pushed back an errant strand of fair hair and boyishly stood to attention.

"Churchill, sir. Winston Churchill. And I promise you, you will hear from me."

CHAPTER FOURTEEN

Y̶ou will forgive my saying so, Holmes, but
your demeanour these past few days has
hardly been that of a man who has pulled off the
biggest coup of his career."

My friend and I were strolling along the
Embankment, having spent the past several
hours at Scotland Yard. The day was bright and
clear as London went about its daily business,
quite unaware—and not for the first time—of
the debt it owed to the man at my side.

"You might fool all the people most of the
time, as I believe one of those American
Presidents was fond of saying," I continued,
"but I know you too well."

"Good old Watson," Holmes gave me a brief
smile, which was soon replaced by a frown.

"No, I must confess that like Hamlet—since
we seem to be exchanging quotations—in my
heart there was a kind of fighting that would
not let me sleep. I have always felt Moriarty as
an elemental force and the vibrations should
have stopped, but they singularly fail to do so.
How do you explain that, good Doctor?"

"But for heaven's sake, Holmes," I riposted,
"we've just seen the man's body."

"We've just seen a cadaver that has been formally identified as Moriarty's body. Conveniently washed up at high tide, wearing clothing of the kind he was wearing, to be sure. Inconveniently so damaged about the head that the face was unrecognisable."

"Probably bumped against the pilings or perhaps a passing boat?" I suggested. "A few days in the water does nothing for a fellow's complexion. I've seen enough of them in my time to know that."

"Possibly, Watson, possibly. And yet . . ."

"And yet—what?"

"I feel we have been thrown a bone, old fellow. Our techniques are still so crude. Some day a pathologist will be able to identify a body without possibility of error by something as small as a single fingerprint, a drop of blood—even its teeth. In some ways we are still groping through the Middle Ages."

As he spoke I had the image of the second gruesome sight we had seen that morning. Steel's corpse had been washed up a day or so earlier much further down river and that contorted face, frozen in a smile of eternal fear, was one I should recall to the end of my days. The denizens of the water had already begun their grim work. Holmes, I noticed, had given the body only a cursory glance. For him Steel was a footnote to history—a fact to be filed in his commonplace book. I wondered which of us had his priorities right.

Then I realised that he was still talking about Moriarty's remains. "But did you not spot the one thing that should give us pause?"

"And what was that, pray?"

"The bullet wound in the shoulder."

"Well, there you are, Holmes, my point precisely. You saw me hit him in that accursed passage way and this morning you saw the medico remove a bullet of exactly the same gauge from the wound. QED."

"*Quod non erat demonstrandum*, I'm afraid. I have never doubted that an Eley's No. 2 was an excellent argument, but the bullet we saw just now was fired from a point considerably nearer than yours. The burn marks on the flesh tell that much. But, more to the point, it was fired *after* death."

Before I could argue, he continued: "You may remember my telling you that in my student days I gained a certain notoriety for conducting experiments which some of my colleagues considered somewhat macabre. They consisted of ascertaining the degree of bruising one could inflict on the corpse. I can assure you the answer is—very little. No, old fellow, this bullet was fired into the arm of a dead man and I very much doubt that his name was Moriarty."

"But why didn't you say something, if you're so sure?"

217

The cold grey eyes left mine and appeared to be searching for something just over the horizon. Whatever it was he sought, I had the clear impression that he saw nothing in between. "This game, whatever it is, is Moriarty's and mine and must be played out as the pieces chance to fall. You are the one person, Watson, I can expect to understand that.

"We have gained the world a breathing space, no more. The forces of unrest that Moriarty sought to tap will not vanish on the breeze. They will find their voice and it will be a harsh voice, I fear—one that will seem to shout down reason for a time. I fear our world has taken its values too much for granted and there are those all too ready to put them to the test. If our way of life prevails—which I hope and pray it shall—it will be stronger and purer for having gone through the flame."

Then, as so often, his mood changed abruptly.

"However, we have achieved something for our efforts, old fellow. We have taken this hand, at least, and Moriarty must think again. The *Clarion* is muted—for good, I suspect. Did you notice the newspaper stand we passed a few minutes ago? Every paper but our friend's seditious medium."

"I should think so, too." I interjected, remembering the scandal of a day or two earlier, when the police had impounded the *Clarion*'s entire morning edition for November 5th with the headline: "PARLIAMENT RISES! HUNDREDS OF MP'S DIE IN NEW GUY FAWKES BLAST! CHAOS GRIPS CAPITAL!" "Tower of London's the place for those fellers."

"Yes, I'm afraid our friend did o'erleap himself a little there."

We walked a little further in companionable silence, then Holmes said—"I suppose it must be admitted that the case was not without its points of interest or, indeed, amusement. The sight of Lestrade tucked away in the cleaning cupboard with a 'Do Not Disturb' sign around his neck will occur to me now every time I see him. At least he retrieved his hat unscathed. That is his one great consolation. And I suppose the fact that, once again, I have allowed the world to believe he solved the case. And I have a feeling that you found at least one other, did you not, Watson?" In someone else his covert glance would have amounted to teasing.

"Do you know, Holmes," I said, straightening my back and pulling in my stomach before I could stop myself, "I do believe I did."

The previous day I had seen Alicia off from King's Cross. In all the publicity surrounding the recent events—in which the other newspapers had self-righteously gone out of their way to castigate Moxton and the *Clarion*—the involvement of a beautiful woman had hardly gone unnoticed. One result of their attention had been a telegram from a woman in Harrogate identifying herself as the estranged sister of Alicia's late mother and now anxious to bind up old wounds. Alicia was to stay with her for a few weeks to regain her health and strength.

As I stood by the closed carriage door, having loaded her with more of everything than she could possibly read or consume on the journey, she leaned out of the open window.

"Dear John, I can never thank you enough, so I am not going to even try. I feel like the little girl in that book who has had the strangest of adventures and then woken up to find that everything is really all right after all. Can you understand that?"

I nodded for I had no words.

"May I ask you one more favour? When I return—for I shall return—I must start my life again. While I am deciding what to do, I have a fancy to try my hand at writing an account of our exploits. I thought I might call it *Alicia's Adventures Under Ground*. You're a writer, John. Will you be my literary advisor?"

"Delighted," I managed to say.

"I should warn you, I'm a slow writer. It may take some time."

And with that she smiled. As the train drew slowly away, it was the smile that remained with me, like that of the most beautiful and benevolent

Cheshire Cat in the world. Holmes interrupted my reverie.

"Well, old fellow, what do you say to a spot of lunch at Rule's before you visit your bookmaker?"

"But how . . . ?"

"Watson, when a man has a copy of the *Pink 'Un*, otherwise known as the *Sporting Times* stuffed in his overcoat pocket, the deduction is hardly a difficult one. However, I do advise you most seriously not to wager heavily on the horse you have selected for the 3:30."

"How can you possibly know what I intend to back in the 3:30?" I demanded.

"The small snort over your Earl Grey at breakfast indicated that you had seen something that intrigued you and when I took the opportunity to glance over your shoulder, I could not help but notice that one of the runners was called The Snark. It seemed to me unlikely in the extreme that, in view of our recent involvement with the works of the late Lewis Carroll, you would be able to resist the coincidence of the reference to *The Hunting of the Snark* . . ."

"By Jove, Holmes, you've read my mind exactly," I declared. "But the horse has got real form. What makes you think it won't win?"

"It cannot win for the simple reason that it doesn't exist." And he began to declaim . . .

He has softly and suddenly vanished away—For the Snark was a Boojum, you see.

"Now, if there happens to be a horse called Boojum, I give you full permission to bet for both of us!"

As we continued walking, his repeated cries of "Come to my arms, my beamish boy! Oh frabjous day! Callooh! Callay!" caused several passers-by to turn and look at him as though he were demented.

And at times like these, I sometimes wonder myself.

Center Point Large Print
600 Brooks Road / PO Box 1
Thorndike, ME 04986-0001 USA

(207) 568-3717

US & Canada:
1 800 929-9108
www.centerpointlargeprint.com

DATE DUE

LP
Day, Barry
Sherlock Holmes and the Alice in
Wonderland Murders